'McBain is so good … *ishers Weekly*

'A virtuoso' *Guardian*

'Ed McBain effectively invented the police procedural … McBain delivers his complex story with panache and real zest … *Money Money Money* may be the fifty-first of the series but it's as fresh and vivid as the first. Great' *Observer*

'Slick, taut, inventive, modern, and (as always) funny' *Glasgow Herald*

'This much-loved and seminal writer is a national treasure. If you're a mystery reader, you've undoubtedly read Ed McBain. If you haven't read one for a while, try this one. It's so good it will immediately send you scurrying back for the ones you missed' Otto Penzler

'A master … as always in his novels, sharp, clear sentences trot briskly one after another … As always, the funny stuff is funny and the scary parts scary. McBain gets it right, of course … as he has done for dozens of books and years' *Time*

'One of the masters of crime fiction' *Sunday Telegraph*

'McBain steadily unrolls a tapestry of adultery, jealousy, and revenge. Amazingly, all the mind-boggling complexities are kept perfectly clear, thanks to McBain's unsurpassed mastery of exposition, the story's still gaining in force when the curtain finally thunders down' *Kirkus Reviews*

'McBain has a great approach, great attitude, terrific style, strong plots, excellent dialogue, sense of place, and sense of reality' Elmore Leonard

'A master storyteller' *Washington Times*

Ed McBain is one of the most illustrious names in crime fiction. In 1998, he was the first non-British author to be awarded the Crime Writers' Association/Cartier Diamond Dagger Award and he is also holder of the Mystery Writers of America's coveted Grand Master Award. His latest novel in Orion paperback is *Fat Ollie's Book*, and his latest hardback novel, *The Frumious Bandersnatch*, is also available from Orion. Visit his website at www.edmcbain.com.

By Ed McBain

THE 87TH PRECINCT NOVELS

Cop Hater • The Mugger • The Pusher • The Con Man
Killer's Choice • Killer's Payoff • Killer's Wedge • Lady Killer
'Til Death • King's Ransom • Give the Boys a Great Big Hand
The Heckler • See Them Die • Lady, Lady, I Did It!
The Empty Hours • Like Love • Ten Plus One
Ax • He Who Hesitates • Doll • Eighty Million Eyes • Fuzz
Shotgun • Jigsaw • Hail, Hail, the Gang's All Here
Sadie When She Died Let's Hear It for the Deaf Man
Hail to the Chief • Bread • Blood Relatives • So Long As You Both Shall Live • Long Time, No See • Calypso • Ghosts • Heat
Ice • Lightning • Eight Black Horses • Poison • Tricks • Lullaby
Vespers • Widows Kiss • Mischief • And All Through the House
Romance • Nocturne • The Big Bad City • The Last Dance
Money, Money, Money • Fat Ollie's Book
The Frumious Bandersnatch

THE MATTHEW HOPE NOVELS

Goldilocks • Rumpelstiltskin • Beauty & the Beast
Jack & the Beanstalk • Snow White and Rose Red • Cinderella
Puss in Boots • The House That Jack Built • Three Blind Mice
Mary, Mary • There Was a Little Girl • Gladly the Cross-Eyed Bear • The Last Best Hope

OTHER NOVELS

The Sentries • Where There's Smoke • Doors • Guns
Another Part of the City • Downtown • Driving Lessons
Candyland • The Moment She Was Gone

KING'S RANSOM

An 87th Precinct novel

Ed McBain

ORION

An Orion paperback

First published in Great Britain in 1962
by T. V. Boardman
Published in Penguin Books 1965
This paperback edition published in 2003
by Orion Books Ltd,
Orion House, 5 Upper St Martin's Lane,
London WC2H 9EA

First published in the USA in 1959
by Simon & Schuster

A CIP catalogue record for this book
is available from the British Library.

Typeset by Deltatype Ltd,
Birkenhead, Merseyside

Printed and bound in Great Britain by
Clays Ltd, St Ives plc

This is for my dear wife, Dragica

The city in these pages is imaginary.
The people, the places are all fictitious.
Only the police routine is based on
established investigatory technique.

1.

THE LONG CURVE of the bay window faced the River Harb and the late-afternoon traffic of tugboats and barges plying their way between the two states. The scene beyond the window was clear with the pristine snappishness of October growing into November, each orange-and-gold leaf boldly shrieking its colour against a sky too blue, too cold.

The room itself was clouded with cigar smoke and cigarette smoke, lacking the sharply defined clarity of the outdoors, hazing over the people who had come to the room to transact business. The smoke hovered on the air like the breath of banished ghosts, clinging like early-morning cemetery mist to the wide hand-pegged planks of the flooring, rising to the exposed hand-hewn timbers in the ceiling. The room was immense, but it was cluttered now with the trivia of an extended skull-cracking session, ash trays over-brimming with butts, used and half-used glasses strewn about the room like the debris of a drunken army in retreat, empty bottles cluttering the tables, the men themselves exhausted and drawn as if they too, like the clinging shifting smoke, were ready to dissipate into the air.

With dogged weariness, the two men sitting opposite Douglas King rapped out their staccato argument with the precision of vaudeville tap dancers. King listened to them silently.

'All we're asking, Doug, is that you think in terms of net profit, that's all,' George Benjamin said.

'Is that a lot to ask?' Rudy Stone said.

'Think of shoes, yes. Don't forget shoes. But only as they apply to net profit.'

'Granger Shoe is a business, Doug, a *business*. Profit and loss. The black and the red.'

'And our job,' Benjamin said, 'is to keep Granger in the black, okay? So keep that in mind, and think of net profit, and then take another look at these shoes.'

He rose from his position in the easy chair. He was a thin waspish man wearing black-rimmed spectacles which overpowered the narrowness of his face. He moved with the swiftness of a bird of prey, walking rapidly, almost gliding to the brass-stemmed, glass-topped teacart which stood some few feet from the sofa. The top of the cart was covered with women's shoes. Benjamin picked up one of these shoes now and, with the same swift gliding movement, a peculiar grace which gave the impression that he was walking several inches above the actual surface of the expensive flooring, walked to where King sat in noncommittal silence. He extended the shoe to him.

'Is that a shoe to stimulate sales?' he asked.

'Don't misunderstand George,' Stone put in hastily. Standing alongside the bookcases which lined one wall of the living room, he looked like nothing less than a Nordic god, muscularly blond, a man of forty-five with all the litheness of an adolescent. He dressed, too, with an arty flair, the checked waistcoat, the off-blue of his sports coat, which seemed too young for his years. 'It's a good shoe, a fine shoe, but we're thinking in terms of net profit now.'

'The red and the black,' Benjamin repeated. 'That's what we're interested in. Am I right, Frank?'

'A hunnerd per cent,' Frank Blake said. He sucked in on his cigar and blew a smoke wreath at the high ceiling.

'This shoe simply doesn't stimulate the masses, Doug,' Stone said, moving away from the bookcases. 'It has no flair.'

'It has no guts,' Benjamin said, 'that's what it hasn't got. Not only can't the average American housewife afford it, she wouldn't buy it even if she *could* afford it. Mrs America, that's who we're after. The little woman who sweats over a hot stove and wipes snotty noses. Mrs America, our customer. Mrs America, the stupidest damn customer in the universe.'

'We've got to excite her, Doug. That's elementary.'

'We've got to bring women to a fever pitch.'

'What excites a woman, Doug?'

'You're a married man. What excites Mrs King?'

King studied Benjamin blandly. Standing some six feet beyond him, mixing a drink at the bar, Pete Cameron looked up suddenly and caught King's eye. He smiled secretly, but King did not return the grin.

'Clothes excite a woman!' Stone said.

'Dresses, hats, gloves, bags, *shoes*!' Benjamin said, his voice rising. 'And shoes are our business, and nobody's in business for his health.'

'But nobody!' Stone said. 'Net profit depends on stimulation, excitement. You can't excite a woman with these shoes. These shoes wouldn't excite a mare in heat!'

The room was silent for a moment.

Then Douglas King said, 'What are we selling? Shoes or aphrodisiacs?'

Frank Blake rose instantly, his thick Southern accent dripping from his thick Southern lips. At fifty-six, he gave the impression of a man who'd been weaned on molasses. 'Doug is makin' a joke,' he said. 'You'll fo'give me, but I din't come all the way from Alabama to hear jokes. I've got money invested in Granger, and from what George Benjamin tells me about how the firm's bein' run, well, I can see why it's almost in the red.'

'Frank is right, Doug,' Benjamin said. 'This is nothing to joke about. Unless we do something fast, Granger Shoe is going to be right up the proverbial creek.'

'Without the proverbial paddle,' Stone added.

'What do you want from me?' King asked softly.

'Now you're asking the right questions,' Benjamin said. 'Pete, let me have another drink, will you?'

From the bar, Cameron nodded. Quickly he began mixing the drink. There was an economy to his motions, as if they too had been pared down to fit the requirements of his well-tailored, grey-flannelled frame. A tall and handsome man of thirty-five, he continued mixing the drink, his brown eyes flicking alternately to each person in the room.

'What do we want from you, Doug?' Benjamin said. 'Okay, here's what we want.'

'Spell it out for him,' Stone said.

Cameron carried the drink over. 'Anybody else?' he asked.

'None fo' me,' Blake said, and he covered the top of his glass.

'You might freshen this one, Pete,' Stone said, handing him his near-empty glass.

'All right, Doug,' Benjamin said. 'In this room, at this moment, we've got the top brains of Granger Shoe, am I right? I represent sales, you represent factory, and Rudy here is fashion co-ordinator. We're all on the board of directors, and we all know damn well what's wrong with the firm.'

'What's that?' King asked.

'The Old Man.'

'His policy is dictating the kind of shoe we produce,' Stone said. 'His policy is driving this company into a hole.'

'He doesn't know a shoe from a corn plaster,' Benjamin said.

'What does he know about women's tastes? What does he know about *women*, for God's sake?' Stone said.

'He's seventy-four years old, and I think he's still a virgin,' Benjamin said.

'But he's president of Granger, and so Granger goes as the Old Man goes,' Stone said.

'But why is he president, Doug? Have you ever stopped to ask yourself that question?'

'Doug isn't a moron, George. He knows why the Old Man's president.'

'Because he has enough votin' stock to swing any election his way,' Blake put in, interrupting the two other men.

'So year in and year out, he's president,' Stone said, nodding.

'And year in and year out, we stand by while he puts out these . . . these *maternity* shoes!' Benjamin said.

'And year in and year out, we watch the company sink into the slime.'

'An' my stock *dee*-preciates in value. Now, tha's no good, Doug.'

Benjamin moved quickly to the teacart. King had been silent while the men spoke. Still silent, he watched Benjamin pick up a red pump from the clutter of shoes on the cart's top.

'Now look at this shoe,' Benjamin said. 'Take a peek at this! Style! Flair! Excitement!'

'I supervised the design of that bitch myself,' Stone said proudly.

'We had samples made up when you were on vacation, Doug.'

'I know what happened at the factory while I was on vacation, George,' King said softly.

'Oh? Oh?'

'Yes.'

'Give him the shoe,' Stone said. 'Let him take a close look.'

Benjamin handed the pump to King and then turned to glance at Blake, who was puffing on his cigar. King turned the shoe over in his big hands, studying it carefully, saying nothing.

'Now how about that, boy?' Benjamin asked. 'The women'll go nuts for that shoe. What do women know, anyway? Do they care about quality, so long as a shoe flatters the foot?'

'I can read his mind,' Stone said. 'He's thinking the Old Man would never let a shoe like that go through.'

'Ah, but the Old Man won't have a thing to say about it, Doug. That's why we're here today.'

'Oh, is that why we're here today?' King asked mildly, but the irony in his voice was lost on everyone but Pete Cameron, who caught it and smiled.

'The Old Man's got a solid chunk of voting stock,' Benjamin said, his eyes narrowing. 'Twenty-five per cent of it.'

'I was wondering when we'd start discussing voting stock,' King said.

Benjamin laughed feebly. 'Oh, this is a shrewd one, Frank,' he said. 'You can't slip anything over on Doug here.'

King did not react to the compliment. In a flat voice he said, 'The Old Man's got twenty-five per cent, and between you, Rudy, and Frank, you've got twenty-one per cent – not enough to take an election from the Old Man.' He paused significantly. 'What's on your mind?'

'Control,' Stone said.

'Control,' Benjamin repeated. 'We want your voting stock. We want you to throw in your voting stock with us.'

'Mmmm?'

'You've got thirteen per cent, Doug. The remainder is scattered around among people who don't give a damn which way an election goes.'

'With your stock, we'll have a neat thirty-four per cent,' Stone said, 'more than enough to override the Old Man. How about it, Doug?'

'Throw in with us, boy,' Benjamin said enthusiastically. 'We'll vote in a new president. We'll put out shoes like the one you're holding in your hand there. We can sell that shoe for seven dollars. We can splash the Granger name all over the low-priced field. The hell with this quality stuff! The big money is with the masses. Invade the low-priced field with a trade name that's always stood for high fashion, and we'll kill the competition.'

'I think George's idea is sound,' Blake drawled. 'I wouldn't've come all the way up here if I dint. I'm interested in protectin' my investment, Doug. Frankly, I don't care *what* kind of shoes we sell, so long as we make money at it. That's *my* business. Makin' money.'

'Vote out the Old Man, huh?' King said. 'Vote in a new president.'

That's right, Doug,' Stone said.

'Who?'

'Who what?'

'Who goes in as president?'

There was a moment of hesitation. The men glanced at each other.

'Naturally,' Stone said, 'you've got thirteen per cent of the stock, and that's considerable, considerable. But at the same time, you can't do anything without our collective chunk, and so . . .'

'I see no reason for pussyfootin' around, Rudy,' Blake said firmly. 'Conversion to the low-priced field was all George's idea, as was this meetin' today. I'm sure Doug will recognize the fairness of our suggestion.'

'We figured,' Stone said cautiously, as if anticipating an explosion, 'that George Benjamin should go in as president.'

'Well now,' King said dryly, 'that's a surprise.'

'With you as executive vice-president, of course,' Stone said hastily, 'at a tremendous salary jump.'

Douglas King studied the men silently for a moment and then slowly rose. Sprawled on the sofa, he had given an impression of stockiness, but as he rose now, the impression was instantly shattered. He was at least six feet two inches tall, with the wide shoulders and narrow waist of an exhibition diver. At forty-two years old, it was doubtful whether or not the greying hair at his temples could be called 'premature.' It nonetheless added a feeling of dignity to the strong hard lines of his cheeks and jaw, the brittle lustre of his blue eyes.

'You'll put out a line like this, is that right, George?' he asked, holding out the red pump. 'You'll use the Granger name on a low-priced shoe?'

'Yes, that's right.'

'Figuring, of course, that we can eliminate perhaps half our normal factory operation.' He hesitated for a fraction of a second, calculating, and then said, 'Stamps and dies would knock out virtually the entire present cutting-room operation. And the machines on the fifth floor would go, and all the—'

'It's a good idea, isn't it, Doug?' Benjamin asked hopefully.

'And this would be the end result. This shoe.' King stared at the pump.

The end result would be a higher net profit,' Blake said.

'Nothing wrong with that shoe, Doug,' Stone said defensively.

'The Old Man may be running us into the ground,' King answered, 'but at least he's always put out an honest shoe. You want to put out garbage.'

'Now just a second, Doug, you wait just a—'

'No, *you* wait just a second! I like Granger Shoe. I've been working in that factory for the past twenty-six years, started in the stockroom when I was sixteen. Aside from the time I spent in the Army, I've been with this firm practically all my adult life. I know every sound and every smell and every operation in that place, and I know shoes. Good shoes. *Quality!* And I won't stick the Granger name on a piece of junk!'

'Well, all right,' Stone said, 'all right, that's just a sample you've got there. We can put out a slightly better shoe. Maybe something to . . .'

'Something to *what*? This shoe'll fall apart in a month! Where's the steel shank in this? Where the hell are the counters? Where's the box toe? What kind of a cheap sock lining is this?' King ripped out the sock lining and then tore off the strap and buckle. With one quick movement of his hands, he snapped off the heel. He held the assembled debris on his hands. 'Is *this* what you're going to sell? To *women*?'

Outraged by the demolition, Stone said, 'That sample cost us—'

'I know exactly what it cost us, Rudy.'

'Romantic notions don't boost profits!' Blake said angrily. 'If we can't make profit with quality, we've got to—'

'*Who* can't make profit with quality?' King asked. 'That'll come as a shock to the other high-fashion houses, all right. Maybe the Old Man can't, and maybe you can't, but—'

'Doug, this is business, business.'

'I know it's business! It's *my* business, the business I love! Shoes are a part of my life, and if I began making garbage my life would begin to smell!'

'I can't continue to hold stock in a firm that's constantly back-sliding,' Blake said. 'That's not sound. That's not . . .'

'Then sell out! What the hell do you want from me?'

'I'd watch the way I was talking, Doug,' Benjamin said suddenly. 'We still control twenty-one per cent, and I've known bigger men than you to be voted out of their jobs.'

'Go ahead, vote me out,' King said.

'If you find yourself out in the street . . .'

'Don't worry about me, George. I'm not going out into any damn street.' He dumped the remains of the red pump onto the teacart and then turned toward the steps which terminated just outside the entrance hall.

'If you helped me become president,' Benjamin said, 'it would mean an enormous salary increase for you. You could—' He stopped abruptly. 'Where do you think you're going? I'm *talking* to you.'

'This is still my house, George,' King said. 'I'm fed up with your meeting, and I'm fed up with your proposition, and I'm fed up with *you*! So I'm leaving. Why don't you follow suit?'

Benjamin walked after him to the steps. His narrow face was flushed with colour now. 'You don't want me to be president of Granger, is that it?' he shouted.

'That's it exactly,' King said.

'Who the hell do you think *should* be president?'

'You just figure it out,' King said, and he went up the steps and out of sight. A deadly silence followed his departure. Benjamin stared up the steps after him, contained anger rising in his face and his eyes. Blake angrily squashed his cigar in an ash tray and then stomped to the hall closet for his coat. Stone began packing the shoes into a sample case, picking up the red shoe scraps gingerly, almost lovingly, shaking his head over the destruction. Finally, Benjamin turned from the stairwell and walked to where Pete Cameron was standing near the bar.

'What's he got up his sleeve, Pete?' he asked.

'His arm, I suppose.'

'Goddammit, don't make jokes! You're his assistant. If anybody knows what he's up to, you do. Now, what is it? I want to know.'

'You're asking the wrong person,' Cameron said. 'I haven't the faintest idea.'

'Then find out.'

'I'm not sure I know what you mean.'

'Don't play it wide-eyed, Pete,' Benjamin said. 'We just offered a plan to Doug. He turned it down cold, in effect told us to go to hell. You don't tell twenty-one per cent of the voting stock to go to hell unless you're feeling mighty strong. Okay, what's he feeling strong about?'

'Why don't you ask *him*?' Cameron said.

'Don't get glib, boy, it's not becoming. What are you making now? Twenty, twenty-five grand? You can make more, Pete.'

'Can I?'

Stone took his coat from the hall closet and walked over to the two men. Pointing back at the staircase, he said, 'If that bastard thinks he's going to get away with this . . .'

'I doan like bein' kicked outa somebody's home,' Blake said angrily. 'I doan like it one damn bit! When's the next Board meetin', George, we're gonna vote Mr High-an'-mighty King right back into the stockroom!'

'He knows that,' Benjamin said softly. 'He knows that, and he doesn't care – and that means he's hooked onto something big. What is it, Pete? A deal with the Old Man?'

Cameron shrugged.

'Whatever it is,' Benjamin said, 'I want it smashed. And whoever helps to smash it may find himself in Douglas King's vacant chair. You know what that chair is worth, Pete?'

'I have some idea.'

'And I've got an idea you know just where you want to go in this company. Think it over, Pete.' Stone handed him his coat and hat. Benjamin put on the coat quickly and then, holding the Homburg in his hands, said, 'Do you know my home number?'

'No.'

'Westley Hills,' Benjamin said. 'That's WE 4–7981. Will you remember it?'

'I've been Doug's assistant for a long time now,' Cameron answered.

'Then it's time you branched out. Give me a call.'

'You're tempting me,' Cameron said, a slight smile on his lips. 'It's a good thing I'm an honourable man.'

The men locked eyes.

'Yes it's a good thing,' Benjamin said dryly. 'That's Westley Hills 4-7981.'

Stone reached down for his sample case, put on his hat and said, 'If that bastard King thinks he can—' and then stopped talking abruptly.

Diane King had come down the steps silently and she stood looking into the room now. The men stared at her speechlessly. Stone was the first to move. He tipped his hat, politely said, 'Mrs King,' and opened the front door.

Benjamin put on his hat. 'Mrs King,' he said politely, and followed Stone out.

Blake dropped his hat, fumbled for it, picked it up, placed it on his balding head, politely said, 'Mrs King,' and hastily left the house, slamming the door behind him.

Immediately Diane said, 'What did they do to Doug?'

2.

THE KING ESTATE – for such it was – lay within the confines of the 87th Precinct. It was, as a matter of fact, at the farthermost reaches of the precinct territory, since nothing lay beyond it but the River Harb. The fallow land of the estate was one section of a parcel which stretched from the river's bend to the arbitrary dividing line of the Hamilton Bridge. Within this parcel, there were perhaps two or three dozen homes which seemed to have been dropped there from another era. Incongruously, they provided the ultra-urban face of the city with an atmosphere at once countrified and other-worldly.

This section of the city was called The Club by everyone in the city except the people who lived there. The residents, of whom there were less than a hundred or so, called it Smoke Rise. They used the title casually, but they knew it represented wealth and exclusiveness; they knew that Smoke Rise was almost a city within a city. Even its geographical location seemed to verify the concept. It was bounded on the north by the River Harb. On its south, the poplars lining the River Highway created a barrier which made Smoke Rise impenetrable from invasion by the rest of the city, the rest of the world.

South of the highway was fancy Silvermine Road, a distantly wealthy (but not *that* wealthy) relative of

Smoke Rise. Continuing Southward from Silvermine Park and the apartment buildings facing it, the peripatetic stroller encountered first the gaudy commercialism, the blinking neons, the all-night restaurants, the candy stores, the shrieking traffic signals of The Stem, crossing the precinct territory like a dagger dripping blood. South of that was Ainsley Avenue, and the change from riches to rags was subtle here, the buildings still maintaining some of their old dignity, the dignity of a once stylish, now shabby Homburg; and then came Culver Avenue and the change was apparent now, striking one in the face with the sudden ferocity of naked poverty, nakedly dirty buildings stretching grime-covered façades to a cold wintry sky, bars crouched between the unemotional masks of tenements, churches huddled on street corners – Come pray to God – the wind sweeping through the grey canyon as bleakly as an icy tundra blast.

Southward, southward, through the short stretch of Mason Avenue known to the Puerto Ricans as La Via de Putas, a flash of exotic colour, a splash of eroticism on the ice floe, and then Grover Avenue and beyond that the happy hunting grounds for muggers, knifers, and rapists, Grover Park.

The 87th Precinct building was on Grover Avenue, facing the park. The detective squadroom was on the second floor of the building.

Detective 2nd/Grade Meyer Meyer sat at a desk before one of the windows overlooking Grover Avenue and the park beyond. The feeble October sunshine reflected from his bald pate, danced in his blue eyes. A pad of lined yellow paper rested on the desk before him.

Meyer scribbled notes onto the pad as the man opposite him spoke.

The man said his name was David Peck. He owned a radio supply store, he told Meyer.

'You sell radio parts, is that right?' Meyer asked.

'Well, not for commercial stuff. I mean, we sell a little of that, but mostly we sell stuff for hams, you know what I mean?' Peck tweaked his nose with his thumb and forefinger. It seemed to Meyer that Peck wanted to blow his nose, or perhaps pick it. He wondered if Peck had a handkerchief. He was going to offer him a Kleenex, but he decided the man might be offended by the gesture.

'Hams?' Meyer said.

'Yeah, hams. I don't mean like you eat. Not them hams.' Peck smiled and tweaked his nose again. 'Like, I mean, we don't run a delicatessen or nothing. By hams, I mean amateur radio operators. Like that. We sell equipment to them mostly. You'd be surprised how many hams there are in this neighbourhood. You wouldn't think so, huh, would you?'

'No, I guess I wouldn't,' Meyer said.

'Sure, lots of hams. My partner and me, we got a pretty good business here. We also sell some commercial stuff, like portables and hi-fi units and like that, but that's only a service we run, you understand, what we are primarily interested in is selling stuff to hams.'

'I understand, Mr Peck,' Meyer said, wishing the man would blow his nose, 'but what is the nature of your complaint?'

'Well,' Peck said, and he tweaked his nose, 'like somebody busted into our store.'

'When was this?'

'Last week.'

'Why'd you wait until now to report it?'

'We wasn't going to report it because the guy who busted in, he didn't steal very much, you know. This equipment is pretty heavy stuff, you know, so I guess you have to be strong to cart away a whole store. Anyway, he didn't take very much, so my partner and me we figured we'd just forget about it.'

'What makes you report it now?'

'Well, he came back. The crook, I mean. The thief.'

'He returned?'

'Yeah.'

'When?'

'Last night.'

'And this time he stole a lot of equipment, is that right?'

'No, no. This time he took even less than last time.'

'Now, just a minute, Mr Peck, let's start from the beginning. Would you like a Kleenex, Mr Peck?'

'A Kleenex?' Peck said. 'What do I need a Kleenex for?' And he tweaked his nose again.

Meyer sighed patiently.

Of all the detectives on the 87th Squad, Meyer Meyer was perhaps the most patient. The patience was not an inherited trait. If anything, Meyer's parents had been capable of behaving somewhat impulsively on occasion. Their first impetuous act involved the conception and birth of Meyer Meyer himself. He was, you see, a change-of-life baby. Now whereas news of an impending birth will generally fill the prospective parents with unrestrained glee, such was not the case when old Max Meyer discovered he was to be presented with an offspring. Max did not take kindly to the news. Not at all. He mulled it over, he stewed about it, he sulked, and finally he decided impulsively upon a means of revenge against the new baby. He named the boy Meyer Meyer, a splendid practical joke, to be sure, a gasser. It almost killed the kid.

Well, perhaps that's exaggeration. After all, Meyer *had* grown to manhood, and he *was* a sound physical and mental specimen. But Meyer had done all his growing in a predominantly Gentile neighbourhood, and the fact that he was an Orthodox Jew with a double-barrelled name like Meyer Meyer did not help him in the winning of friends or the influencing of people. In a neighbourhood where the mere fact of Jewishness was enough to provoke spontaneous hatred, Meyer Meyer had had his troubles. 'Meyer Meyer, Jew on fire,' the kids would chant, and whereas they never translated the chant into an actual conflagration, they committed everything short of arson against the Jewboy with the crazy monicker.

Meyer Meyer learned to be patient. You couldn't win a fight against a dozen other boys by using your fists. You learned to use your head instead. Patiently, intelligently, Meyer Meyer handled his problem without the aid of a psychiatrist. Patience became an ingrown trait. Patience became a way of life. So perhaps old Max Meyer's joke was harmless enough. Unless one cared to make note of the fact that Meyer Meyer was as bald as a cue ball. And even this fact assumed no real importance until it was connected with a second purely chronological fact:

Meyer Meyer was only thirty-seven years old.

Patiently now, he poised his pencil over the yellow

pad and said, 'Tell me, Mr Peck, what did this thief steal the first time he broke into your store?'

'An oscillator,' Peck said.

Meyer made a note on his pad. 'How much does the oscillator sell for?' he asked.

'Well, this is a six-hundred-volt oscillator, number 2L-2314. We sell it for fifty-two dollars and thirty-nine cents. That's including tax.'

'And that's all he took the first time?'

'Yes, that's all he took. We get a forty per cent markup on the item, so our loss wasn't really that big. So we decided like to forget about it, you know?'

'I see. But the thief broke into your store again last night, is that correct?'

'That is correct,' Peck said, tweaking his nose.

'And what did he steal this time?'

'Little items. Like a relay which we sell for ten dollars and twenty-two cents, including tax. And some batteries. And a knife switch. Things like that. He couldn't have swiped more than twenty-five bucks' worth of equipment.'

'But this time you're reporting it?'

'Yes.'

'Why? I mean, if the loss this time was smaller than the loss . . .'

'Because we're afraid he might come back a third time. Suppose he comes back with a goddamn truck and cleans out the store? It's possible, you know.'

'I know it is. And we appreciate your reporting the crimes to us, Mr Peck. We'll keep a special watch on your store from now on. Would you give me the name of it, please?'

'Pecker Parts,' Peck said.

Meyer blinked. 'Uh . . . where'd you get that name?' he asked.

'Well, my last name is Peck, as you know.'

'Yes.'

'And my partner's first name is Erwin. So we put the two names together and we got Pecker Parts.'

'Wouldn't you have done better by using some other portion of your partner's name? His last name perhaps?'

'His last name?' Peck said. 'I really don't see how we could have used that.'

'What *is* his last name?'

'Lipschitz.'

'Well,' Meyer said, and he sighed. 'And what is the address of the store, Mr Peck?'

'Eighteen twenty-seven Culver Avenue.'

'Thank you,' Meyer said. 'We'll keep an eye on it.'

'Thank *you*,' Peck said. He rose, tweaked his nose, and left the squadroom.

The theft of equipment amounting to a loss of some seventy-five dollars was certainly not important in itself. Or, at least, not important as thefts go, unless you're a stickler for the letter of the law, one of those people who insist that *any* silly little theft is really crime. In the 87th Precinct, however, seventy-five-dollar losses were commonplace, and if you knocked yourself out tracking down every bit of petty larceny, you'd have no time left for the really serious crimes being committed. No, on the face of it Mr Peck's paltry pilfering complaint was nothing to get all excited about – unless you happened to be a man named Meyer Meyer who kept abreast of what was happening around him in the squadroom and in the precinct and who was blessed with a fairly retentive memory.

Meyer studied the notes on the pad before him and then walked over to a desk on the other side of the room. Steve Carella was sitting at that desk, busily typing up a report, the forefingers of both hands beating the typewriter into reluctant submission.

'Steve,' Meyer said. 'I just had a guy in here who—'

'Shhh, shhh,' Carella said, and he continued banging away at the machine until he finished his paragraph. Then he looked up.

'Okay?' Meyer said.

'Shoot.'

'I just had a guy in here who—'

'Why don't you sit down? You want some coffee? Let's get Miscolo to make some coffee.'

'No, I don't want any coffee,' Meyer said patiently.

'This isn't a social visit?'

'No. I just had a guy in here who owns a radio parts store on Culver Avenue.'

'Yeah?'

'Yeah. So the store was broken into twice in a row. The first time the thief stole an oscillator, whatever the hell that is, and the second time just a bunch of loose junk hanging around. Now it seems to me I remember . . . '

'Yeah, how about that?' Carella said. He shoved the typing cart away from the desk and opened his bottom drawer. Dumping a sheaf of papers on the desk top, he began rifling through them hurriedly.

'A whole bunch of radio store burglaries, weren't they?' Meyer said.

'Yeah, yeah,' Carella answered. 'Where the hell's that list?' He continued scattering papers over the desk top. 'Look at this. More junk in this damn drawer. This guy was caught and is already serving his time at Castleview. Now where's that ... ? Jewellery stores ... bicycles ... Why doesn't somebody add these to the stolen-bikes file? ... Here it is. This the thing you were referring to?'

Meyer looked at the typewritten sheet.

'That's it,' he said. 'Pretty strange, don't you think?'

There was, in truth, nothing strange about the list. It simply enumerated the amount of equipment that had been stolen from several different radio parts stores over the past several months. Both men bent over the list (*overleaf*) and studied it more closely.

'What do you make of it?' Meyer said.

'I don't know.'

'Well, you must have thought there was something fishy, or you wouldn't have scribbled that note to the lieutenant.'

'Yeah,' Carella said.

'What did Pete have to say about it?'

'Not a hell of a lot. Figured it was some kids, I think.'

'What was the m.o., Steve? Do you remember?'

'A window at the back of the shop was forced in each case. And in each case, only one large item or a few small items were stolen.'

'Why do you suppose the thief did that?'

'Maybe he figured a small theft wouldn't be reported. Or perhaps not even missed. Assuming this was the same thief on each job.'

'Well, it sure as hell looks that way to me,' Meyer said.

'Mmm. In any case, it's not very serious.'

'I suppose not. Here. You'd better add these new ones

RADIO EQUIPMENT THEFTS

DATE REPORTED	SHOP AND ADDRESS	EQUIPMENT	SERIAL NUMBER
June 11th	David Radio, 312 N. 10	Oscillator 1600 volt	216-81-R 17
		Dial	
		Battery	
July 22nd	R&L Parts, 4511 Mason Avenue	Transmitter 35.66 mg.	TX 11-4812
August 5th	Sparks, Inc. 7614 Grover Avenue	Receiver 43.66 mg.	RV 327-89L
September 8th	OSIKRIAS ~~Osigies~~ Radio Parts, Repair & Service, South 14th and Culver	four relays (one inch by three inch)	
		six Batteries	
		thirty-five-ft. rubberized wire	

PETE:
M.O. SAME ON THESE.
MAKE ANY CONNECTION?
Steve

to your list.' Meyer paused and scratched his bald head. 'You suppose we're dealing with a Russian spy or something here?'

'Either that or a member of the I.R.A.'

'I mean, why else would anybody want all these parts?'

'We may be dealing with a ham who can't afford his hobby,' Carella said.

'Yeah, so why doesn't he switch his hobby?'

'One thing I stopped worrying about the minute I became a detective,' Carella said, 'is motive. If you try to figure out what motivates a crook, you go nuts.'

'You're destroying a boy's faith in detective fiction,' Meyer said. 'The Means, the Motive, and the Opportunity. Everybody knows that.'

'Except me. I just do my job,' Carella said.

'Yeah,' Meyer said.

'It always comes out in the wash, anyway. One day, all the mysterious pieces click together. And they're never what you thought they were going to be. To figure out motivation, you have to be a psychiatrist.'

'Still,' Meyer said, 'all that equipment. And the thief hit seven times to get it. That's a big chance to take for a hobby. What does it add up to, Steve?'

'Beats the hell out of me,' Carella said, and he began typing again.

3.

DIANE KING WAS not a beautiful woman.

She was, however, an attractive woman.

Her attractiveness was directly attributable to the bone structure of her face, which, while not adding up to the Hollywood or Madison Avenue concept of beauty, nonetheless provided an excellent foundation upon which to build. Her attractiveness, too, was indirectly attributable to a number of things like: (a) the various concoctions offered by the myriad beauty-preparation firms, (b) a life of comparative ease and luxury, (c) ready access to the hairdresser's, and (d) an innate good taste in the selection of clothes to complement a figure unendowed with a movie star's mammillary overabundance.

Diane King was attractive. Diane King, in fact, was damned attractive.

She stood just inside the entrance foyer of her luxurious home, a woman of thirty-two wearing black tapered lounging slacks and a long-sleeved white blouse open at the throat. A towel was draped over the neck and shoulders of the blouse. Her hair echoed the ebony black of the slacks, except for a fresh silver streak which rose from a widow's peak and spread like mercury to a point somewhere on the top of her head. A silver-studded belt circled her narrow waist. Her green eyes fled from the entrance doorway to Pete Cameron's face, and again she asked, 'What did they do to Doug?'

'Nothing,' Cameron said. He looked at her hair. 'What'd *you* do to your hair?'

Distractedly, Diane's hand went up to the silver streak. 'Oh, it was Liz's idea,' she said. 'What was all the shouting about, Pete?'

'Is Liz still here?' Cameron asked, and there was an undeniable note of interest in his voice.

'Yes, she's still here. Why'd Doug come steaming upstairs like the Twentieth Century? I hate these damn high-power meetings. He didn't even *see* me up there, Pete, do you know that?'

'He saw *me*,' a voice said, and Liz Bellew came down the steps and into the living room. Whatever Diane King lacked in the way of beauty, Liz Bellew possessed. She was born with blonde hair that needed no hairdresser's magic, blue eyes fringed with thick lashes, an exquisitely moulded nose and a pouting sultry mouth. She had acquired over the years a figure which oozed S-E-X in capital letters in neon, and had overlaid – if you'll pardon the expression – her undeniable beauty with a polish as smooth and as hard as baked enamel. Even dressed for casual life in Smoke Rise, as she was now, wearing simple sweater and skirt, suede flats, and carrying a suede pouch-like bag, sex dripped from her curvaceous frame in bucketfuls, tubfuls, vatfuls. She wore only one piece of jewellery, a huge diamond on her left hand, a diamond the size of a malignant cancer.

'I'll be damned if I'll let *any* man rush past Liz Bellew without saying hello,' she said, obviously referring to her encounter with King upstairs.

'So hello,' Cameron said.

'I was wondering when you'd notice me.'

'I understand you've turned beautician in your spare time,' Cameron said.

'Diane's hair! Isn't it stunning?'

'I don't like it,' Cameron said. 'Forgive my honesty. I think she's quite beautiful without any gilding of the lily—'

'Oh, hush, monster,' Liz said. 'The streak gives her glamour. It emancipates her.' She paused. Underplaying the next line, she said. 'Besides, she can wash it out if she doesn't like it.'

'Well, I'll see what Doug thinks first,' Diane said.

'Darling, never ask a man what he thinks about any part of your body. Am I right, Pete?'

Cameron grinned. 'Absolutely.'

Diane glanced toward the steps nervously. 'What's he *doing* up there?'

'Your beloved?' Liz said. 'He's only making a phone call. I stopped him, and he apologized for ignoring me, and said he had an important call to make.'

'Pete, are you sure he's not in trouble? That look on his face . . .'

'Don't you know that look?' Liz said. 'My God, Harold wears it all the time. It simply means he's about to murder someone.'

'Murder?'

'Certainly.'

Diane turned sharply to Cameron. 'Pete, what happened down here?'

Cameron shrugged. 'Nothing. They offered Doug a deal, and he spit in their collective eye.'

'My Harold would have kicked them out of the house,' Liz said.

'That's just what Doug did.'

'Then everything's under control. Prepare for a homicide, Diane.'

'I'm always prepared for one,' Diane said. A troubled look had come into her green eyes. She turned away from Liz and Cameron and walked to the bar. 'But they seem to be getting more and more frequent.'

'Well, Diane,' Cameron said, 'that's business. Dog eat dog.'

'Anyway, murder can be fun,' Liz put in. 'Lay back and enjoy it, that's my motto.' She smiled archly at Cameron, who immediately returned the smile.

If there seemed to be slightly more than ultrasophisticated social palaver between Cameron and Liz, if indeed they seemed to have shared more than a passing acquaintanceship, the impression was probably nurtured by the fact that they had, over the years, and discreetly, to be sure, enjoyed that boat ride up extramarital waters. For whereas Liz Bellew was devoted to her husband Harold, and whereas Pete Cameron was a junior executive whose every waking moment was occupied with thoughts of the company, they had each managed to find the time to be mutually attracted, to arrange a first tentative meeting, and then to fall into a pattern of assignations which bordered on bacchanals.

Liz Bellew was suffering from a disease known to many thirty-five-year-old women and labelled by medical science 'itchiness.' It was all well and good to be married to a successful tycoon, and it was marvellous to live in Smoke Rise with an upstairs maid, a downstairs maid and a chauffeur, and it was delightful to be able to wear mink interchangeably with ermine – but when something like Pete Cameron strolled by, the temptation to add another acquisition to the Bellew holdings was not easily put aside. Nor was Liz a person who really struggled too valiantly against the siren calls of everyday living. Lay back and enjoy it, that was her motto. And she'd been doing just that for as long as she could remember. Happily, Pete Cameron satisfied her about as well as any mere thing of flesh and blood could satisfy her, and – thanks to him – she was saved the ugliness of becoming a real wanton. In any case, their public face, a mask they had both agreed to wear, consisted of a light sex play designed to evoke in the viewer and listener the feeling that there could not possibly be any fire where there was so much obvious smoke.

Diane poured herself a drink and turned to face Cameron. '*Is* Doug planning to slit another throat?' she asked.

'Yes, I think so.'

'I thought after what he did to Robinson, he might just possibly . . .'

'Robinson?' Liz said. 'Oh, yes, that quaint little man. He played lousy bridge. Doug's better off without him.'

'I'm better off without *whom*?' King asked from the staircase, and then he came down the steps exuberantly and walked directly to Diane where she stood near the bar.

'Did you make your call, tycoon?' Liz asked.

'The lines are tied up,' King answered. He kissed his wife lightly, backed away from her with a small take, and studied the silver streak in her hair. 'Honey,' he said, 'you've got egg in your hair.'

'Sometimes I wonder why we bother,' Liz said sourly.

'Don't you like it, Doug?' Diane asked.

King weighed his answer carefully. Then he said, 'It looks kind of cute.'

'Holy God, it looks kind of cute!' Liz mimicked. 'The last time I heard that was at a senior tea. From a football player named Leo Raskin. Do you remember him, Diane?'

'No. I didn't know many football players.'

'I wore a blouse cut down to—' Liz paused and then indicated a spot somewhere close to her abdomen – 'well, at least *here*! I was practically naked, believe me, it's a wonder I wasn't expelled from college. I asked Leo for his opinion, and he said, "It looks kind of cute." '

'What's wrong with that?' King asked.

'*It* looks kind of cute?' Liz said. 'Hell, even a football player should be able to *count*!' She glanced quickly at her watch. 'I'm getting out of here. I promised *my* tycoon I'd be back by four.'

'You're late already,' Cameron said. 'Have one for the road.'

'I really shouldn't,' Liz said, and she smiled at him archly.

'*Two* lemon peels?'

'The memory on that boy. He knows I can't resist his cocktails.'

Her eyes locked with Cameron's. Neither Diane nor King paid the slightest bit of attention to all this obvious smoke. Happily, the telephone rang, and Diane picked it up.

'Hello?' she said.

'Ready on your call to Boston now,' the operator said.

'Oh, thank you. Just a moment, please.' She handed the phone to King. 'Were you calling Boston, Doug?'

'Yes,' he said, taking the receiver.

Cameron looked up from the Martinis he was mixing. 'Boston?'

'Hello?' King said into the phone.

'We're ready with your Boston call now, sir. One moment, please.' There was a long pause, and then the operator said, 'Here's your party, sir.'

'Hello?' a voice asked. 'Hello?'

'Is that you, Hanley?' King asked.

'Yes, Doug, how are you?'

'Fine. How's it going up there?'

'Just about the way we expected, Doug.'

'Well, look, we've got to sew this thing up fast.'

'How fast?'

'Today,' King said.

'Why? Something wrong?'

'I just had the undertakers in here for a showdown,' King said, 'and they're not going to sit still for very long. What's with our man anyway?'

'He wants to hang on to five per cent, Doug.'

'What? What the hell for?'

'Well, he feels—' Hanley started.

'Never mind, I'm not interested. That five per cent is as important to me as the rest of it, so get it. Just get it, Hanley!'

'Well, I'm trying my best, Doug, but how can I . . . ?'

'I don't give a damn how you do it, just do it! Go back to him, cry on his shoulder, hold his hand, go to bed with him, get what we want!'

'Well, it may take a little time,' Hanley said.

'How *much* time?'

'Well . . . actually, I don't know. I suppose I can go over to see him right now.'

'Then go ahead. And call me back as soon as you've seen him. I'll be waiting. And listen, Hanley, I'll assume you're going to deliver and I'll act accordingly. So don't foul me up. Do you understand?'

'Well, I'll try.'

'Don't just try, Hanley. Succeed. I'll be waiting for your call.' He hung up and turned to Cameron. 'Pete, you're going to Boston.'

'I am?' Cameron said. He handed the Martini to Liz.

'How lucky you are!' she said. 'I just adore Scollay Square.'

'You're going to Boston with a big fat cheque,' King said, 'and you're going to deliver that cheque to Hanley, and we're going to close the biggest damn deal I've ever made in my life!'

'If your lawyer's in on it, it must be big,' Cameron said. 'What's it all about, Doug?'

'Now don't jinx it,' King said smiling. 'I don't like to talk about anything until it's all set. I'll tell you all about it in due time, but not until I'm sure, okay? Meanwhile, you get on the phone and find out how the flights are running to Boston. Use the upstairs phone. I want to leave this line clear for Hanley.'

'Sure, Doug,' Cameron said, and he started for the steps. He stopped, turned toward Liz and said, 'You won't leave without saying goodbye, will you?'

Liz looked up from her Martini. 'Darling, I *always* linger over my farewells,' she said.

Cameron smiled and went up the steps. King clapped

his hands together once, sharply, and began pacing the room.

'Oh, are those vultures going to be surprised! They think they're circling a dead body, but watch their faces when the body stands up and smacks them in the teeth! Asking *me* to go in with *them*, can you beat that, Diane?'

'Excuse me, Mr King,' a voice said.

The man who had come in at the other end of the living room could not have been more than thirty-five years old, but at first glance he appeared much older. It was, perhaps, the way he stood hesitantly in the doorway to the living room, his shoulders hunched, the chauffeur's uniform adding somehow to his posture of demeanour. His name was Charles Reynolds, but he was called simply Reynolds by everyone in the King household, and perhaps a man reduced to his last name is a man driven to his last retreat. Whatever the case, there was an almost tangible weakness about the man. Watching him, you felt you could reach out and touch a substance at once sticky and gelatinous. And watching him, too, you felt an extreme sympathy, a sadness. Even if you did not know his wife had died not a year ago, even if you did not know he shared the rooms over the King garage with his young son, raising the boy with the awkwardness of bereavement – even unaware of this, you felt sympathy for the man, you felt he was one of the world's strays.

'What is it, Reynolds?' King asked.

'Excuse me, sir, I didn't mean to intrude.'

'You're not intruding,' King said. There was a gruffness to his voice. Fond of the man as he was, King could not abide weakness, and weakness was this man's strength.

'I only wanted to know, sir . . . is my son . . . is Jeff here, sir?'

'That's *Mrs* King's department,' King said.

'He's upstairs with Bobby, Reynolds.'

'Oh, fine. I hope I'm not bothering you, ma'am, but it's turned a little chilly, and I figured he might need a coat if he goes outside to play.'

Diane studied the overcoat in Reynolds' hands with a practised mother's eye. 'I think that might be a little heavy, Reynolds. I've already given him one of Bobby's sweaters.'

Reynolds looked at the coat as if seeing it for the first time. 'Oh . . .' He smiled sheepishly. 'Well, thank you, ma'am. I never can seem able to decide what . . .'

'You'll probably be driving Mr Cameron to the airport, later,' King cut in. 'Plan on that, will you?'

'Yes, sir. When will we be leaving, sir?'

That's not definite yet. I'll buzz you when we know.'

A bloodcurdling scream erupted from someplace upstairs, followed by a second more chilling one, and followed immediately by the thunder of elephant hoofs on the stairs. Bobby King, wearing a blue sweater, his blond hair hanging over his forehead, charged down the steps with Jeff Reynolds in hot pursuit. At first glance, the boys seemed to be brothers. They were both blond, both of the same height and build, both carrying toy rifles, and both screaming in the same high voices. They were, however, both eight years old and did not really resemble each other in the slightest except for their build and colouration, ergo the brother concept was instantly shattered unless one admitted the possibility of their being fraternal twins. Whooping and yelling, they headed for the front door, ignoring everyone in the living room.

'Hey!' King shouted, and his son pulled up an imaginary horse.

'Whoa, boy, whoa!' Bobby said. 'What is it, Dad?'

'Where're you going?'

'Outside to play,' Bobby said.

'How about a good-bye?'

'*Good-bye*,' Liz Bellew said, rising and rolling her eyes. 'This is beginning to resemble *my* menagerie.'

'We're in an awful hurry, Dad,' Bobby said.

'Why? Where's the fire?'

'There's no fire, Mr King,' Jeff said, 'but we've got a game to play.'

'Oh? What kind of a game?'

'Creeks,' Jeff said.

'What's that?'

'It's what I'll be up unless I get home soon,' Liz said.

'It's Injuns,' Jeff explained. 'Creeks are Injuns, don't you know?'

'Oh, I see.'

'We take turns bein' Creek,' Bobby said. 'We got to find each other in the woods. When I'm the cavalry . . .'

'Oh, God, this is really all too familiar,' Liz said. 'I *must* go.'

'. . . and Jeff's a Creek, I got to find him. When I capture him . . .'

'Is that what all the artillery's for?' King asked, indicating the toy rifles each of the boys carried.

'Sure,' Bobby said solemnly. 'You can't go in the woods unarmed, can you?'

'I should say not.'

'Don't go too far from the house, Bobby,' Diane said.

'I won't, Mom.'

'Who's the Creek now?' King asked.

'I am!' Jeff said, and he let out a war whoop and began dancing around the room.

'Jeff!' Reynolds cried sharply, embarrassed.

'I'm doin' the ceremonial,' his son explained.

'Don't shout so. And take good care of the sweater Mrs King loaned you.'

'Oh, sure,' Jeff said, glancing at the bright-red sweater cursorily. 'He won't catch me, Dad, don't worry.'

'I don't care whether he catches you or not, just so—'

'Oh, won't he now?' King interrupted. 'You'd *better* catch him, son. The family name's at stake.'

'I'll get him,' Bobby said, grinning.

'What's your strategy?' King asked.

'Huh?'

'Your plan.'

'Just chase him and catch him, that's all.' Bobby shrugged.

'Never chase the other fellow, son,' King advised. 'That's no way to do it. I can see you need help.'

'Oh, Doug, let them go play before it gets dark,' Diane said.

'I will,' King said, smiling, 'but the boy needs assistance from a professional scalp hunter, can't you see that? Come here, Bobby.' He took his son aside so that Jeff could not hear the conversation. Whispering, he said, 'Climb up a tree, see? Watch him from up there. Watch everything he does. You're holding all the cards that way because he doesn't know just where you are. Then, when you're certain of what he's about to do, beat him to the punch. Pounce!'

'Doug!' Diane said sharply.

'You weren't supposed to be listening, hon,' King said.

'But climbing trees is against the rules of the game, Dad,' Bobby said.

'Make your own rules!' King said. 'So long as you win.'

'Doug, what in the world are you telling him?' Diane said.

'Only the facts of life, I'd suspect,' Liz answered.

'All they want to do, you know, is get outside and start their game.'

'How come I don't get any help?' Jeff said, turning to his father. 'What should I do, Dad?'

Reynolds, caught by surprise, obviously embarrassed in the presence of his employer, said, 'Well . . . uh . . . you can lie flat behind a rock. He'd never find you that way.'

'Unless you move, Jeff,' King said. 'Then, brother, watch out!'

'But if you don't move, son, you're safe,' Reynolds said with seeming logic.

'If nobody moves, there's no game,' King said. 'What's the sense in playing?'

'I think you'd do best, boys, to play the game just the way you want to,' Diane said, somewhat coldly. 'Go on now, have fun.'

The war whoops erupted again, the rifles were once more brandished in the air. The red sweater and the blue sweater moved in a purplish blur toward the front door, and the ensuing slam shook the house.

'Wow!' Liz said.

'I'll have the car ready whenever Mr Cameron needs it, sir,' Reynolds said.

'Fine,' King said, mentally dismissing Reynolds even before he had left the room.

'Thank you, sir,' Reynolds said, and he backed into the dining room and then turned and walked into the shadows toward the kitchen.

Diane waited until she was sure he was gone. Then she said, 'You shouldn't have told him that, Doug.'

'Huh? Told who what?'

'To . . . to climb a tree and watch and then pounce. Make your own rules! Win at any cost! What are you trying to raise? A jungle tiger?'

'Mmmm, yes,' King said, 'like his mother. Flashing eyes and sharp teeth and—'

'Doug, I'm serious!'

'Darling, so is he,' Liz said shrewdly. 'He's making love to you, can't you tell? I'd better go.'

'What kind of nonsense is that to tell a boy?' Diane said angrily. 'Pounce! For the love of— Do you want . . . do you want him to grow up to be a . . . a . . . ?'

'A rapist?' Liz supplied.

'Yes, thank you, Liz.'

'Why not?' King said. 'Like father, like . . .'

'I'm terribly sorry you think this is a joke. I don't happen to see anything so funny about it.'

Liz Bellew sighed. 'Methinks I see a storm warning for Hurricane Diane,' she said.

'Don't be silly,' Diane said with utter composure. 'You've known me long enough to tell when I'm angry or not.' She allowed her fury to smoulder silently for a moment longer and then exploded. 'Pounce, pounce,

pounce! The way you're doing with this Boston thing, the way you did with poor Robinson!'

'*Poor* Robinson?' King said.

'Yes, you know very well what I mean.'

'I fired a man. What's so criminal about that?'

'Harold fires men every day,' Liz said brightly.

'Of course,' King said. 'Honey, when you're in business, you can't worry about . . .'

'Yes, but *why* did you fire him? And *how*? The Robinsons were our friends.'

'Friends? Because we had them in for bridge a few times?'

'It wasn't a few times, and they were our friends!'

'All right, they *were* our friends. They're not any more.' King paused. 'He was making me look bad.'

'And is that a reason for . . .'

'Look, I told you he was charging sales trips to the cost of a shoe. Some idiot goes to Italy to buy silk, and Robinson charges that up to Cost. He was making me and the factory end look sick. He was being unfair, and I asked him repeatedly to re-evaluate his system. You know he refused.'

'So you fired him. You didn't even give him the chance to resign.'

Liz Bellew, apparently bored by the kind of talk she heard endlessly in her own house, stretched out on the couch and glanced at the staircase.

'Resign?' King said. 'The hell with resignation! When a man isn't doing his job right . . .'

'What happens when he looks for another job, when he has to tell a prospective employer he was *fired*?'

'Only a damn fool would say he was fired. If Robinson has any sense at—'

'You know they'll check with Granger, no matter what he says.'

'Well, he should have thought of that before he began holding hands with the Sales Division. Diane, he was knocking Cost 'way the hell out of line!'

'You didn't have to be so *ruthless*!'

'Ruthless? Me?' He laughed. 'Liz, am I ruthless?'

'You're a darling,' Liz said.

'What makes you think I'm ruthless? Because I get things done while other people sit around on their fannies? Honey, there are sitters and there are doers. Just because a man takes action doesn't necessarily mean . . .'

'No, but if you make a habit of stepping on people, of not caring . . .'

'Honey, if I'd sat on my duff all these years, you wouldn't be living in this house right now, you wouldn't be wearing that bracelet, you . . .'

'He's right, darling,' Liz said, and she extended the hand with the diamond on it.

'Of course I am. You either *do* or you *sit*, right, Liz?'

'Absolutely,' Liz said. She swung upright. 'I've always enjoyed a little action myself.' She looked at her watch. 'Well, back to the little shack on the hill for me. You two coming to the club tonight?'

'Maybe,' Diane said angrily.

'Mmmm.' Liz stared at Diane. 'I know what *she* needs,' she said to King.

'So do I.'

'I figured you did. By the way, if Pete asks—' She cut herself off. 'Never mind, he's a big boy now.' She waved her hand, called, 'Have fun,' and walked out of the house.

There was a dead silence after her departure. Diane stood stockstill in the centre of the room. King studied her for a moment and then began circling her slowly.

'Diane?' he said gently.

'What is it?'

'Diane, I'm sitting in a tree, and I'm looking down at you . . .'

'What?' she said, puzzled.

Circling closer, King said, 'And I'm warning you now . . . in all fairness . . . that I am getting ready to . . . *pounce*!'

He seized her suddenly, holding her close to him, his mouth an inch from hers.

'Let me go!' she said. 'If you think you can—' and King kissed her. She struggled for a moment longer, and then submitted to his kiss, and then returned it, clinging to him, and then pulled her mouth from his.

'You . . . you oaf,' she said gently.

'Yes,' he said, and he kissed her again.

'You are,' she said weakly. 'You should be ashamed of yourself.'

'I am. Deeply.' He kissed her again. 'You're beautiful. Especially with that new sexy streak in your hair.'

'I'm too good for you, that's for sure, you ape.'

'I know, I know. Listen, what time's dinner?'

'Why?' she asked suspiciously.

'I thought we might . . .' He shrugged.

'And I didn't appreciate your discussing me with Liz as if I were a head of cattle or something.'

'Mmmm, you're a gorgeous head of cattle,' he said, and again he kissed her. 'You didn't answer me.'

'What did you ask?' Diane said dizzily.

King kissed her neck. 'Dinner,' he whispered. 'The time before dinner.'

'Pete's wandering around the house, you know.'

'I'll get rid of him. I'll fire him.'

'How can you . . . ?'

'I'll send him out to the airport early.'

'Well . . .' Diane said hesitantly.

'Well?'

'Well . . .' An embarrassed smile formed on her mouth.

'Good!' King said. 'Let me check with Hanley first.'

'Check with Hanley!'

'I mean, I don't want him calling back in the . . .'

'Maybe I should arrange this through your secretary,' Diane said.

King grinned and slapped her on the rump as he went to the phone. He picked up the receiver, turned toward her, and said, 'This'll only take a minute. All I want to do is—' He stopped suddenly, aware that someone else was on the line, and then recognizing the voice as Cameron's.

'. . . yes, George,' Cameron was saying, 'that's what I'm trying to tell you. Well, I thought you'd like to know . . .'

Hastily, King pushed a button in the base of the phone, switching to another line. 'Funny,' he said.

'What's the matter?' Diane asked.

'Pete's on the other line,' King said. There was a puzzled look on his face. 'I could've sworn he was talking to . . .' He shrugged, dialled the operator and waited. 'Think you can get me Oscar Hanley at the Hotel Stanhope in Boston?' he said. He listened for a moment. 'All right, call me back, will you?' He hung up and turned toward his wife. 'In the meantime, my dear, how about a little drink to—'

The front door burst open. The Creeks were returning. Or at least one of the Creeks.

'Bobby, don't come barging into the house like that!' Diane shouted at her son as he charged up the steps to the bedroom area.

'Sorry, Mom! I forgot my powder horn! Where is it, Mom?'

'Upstairs in your toy chest, where it usually is.'

'Help me find it, will you?'

'You know where it is.'

'Yeah, but I'm in a hurry,' Bobby said. 'Jeff's already got a head start, and I-hey! There it is! Hanging on my doorknob!' He let out a wild whoop and stomped down the corridor, to return a moment later with the powder horn slung over his shoulder. 'So long!' he yelled. 'I got to find myself a tree, Dad!' and he stormed out of the house again.

'Wait,' Diane said reproachfully, 'and then pounce.'

The man in the bushes was waiting to pounce.

He was dying for a cigarette, but he knew he dared not light one. From his hidden vantage point, he could see the windowless side of the King house and the entrance to the garage. The long black Cadillac was parked in the driveway, and a chauffeur was running a chamois cloth over the sleek hood of the automobile. The man in the bushes glanced at the chauffeur, and then at his watch, and then at the sky. It would be dark soon. Good. Darkness was what they needed.

He wished for a cigarette.

He wondered if Eddie was still with the car. He

wondered if everything was okay at the house. He wondered if the whole thing would work, and, wondering about it, he began to worry about it, and his palms got damp and he wanted a cigarette more than ever.

He heard a noise in the bushes, and he felt fear crackle up his spine to explode inside his skull like a yellow sky-rocket.

Cool, he told himself. *Cool*.

He forced his hands to stop trembling by clenching them tightly. He squeezed his eyes shut, and then opened them again, and then saw the figure coming through the woods, and his heart gave a sudden lurch. It was the boy.

He wet his lips.

When his voice came from his mouth, it came as a hoarse cracked sound. He swallowed hard and tried again.

'Hi, sonny,' he said. 'What you doing? Playing cops and robbers?'

Dusk was beginning to shoulder its way into the city.

In October there is a special feel to dusk, the softness of a cat's muzzle, and it is accompanied by the smell of wood smoke even in the heart of the city where people do not burn wood or leaves. The smell is something ingrained on the race memory of man, and it lends a quality of serenity to October which no other month can claim. The street lamps go on a little before darkness really falls. The sun stains the sky with a brilliant red, interlaced with the solemn purple of a vault of clouds wheeling heavenward. The bridges span the city in bold silhouette, suspended cables backdropped by the stain of purple dusk, green lights winking in the coming darkness like strung emeralds.

The pace quickens a little, the step becomes a little lighter. There is a briskness on the air, and it bites the cheeks and stings the teeth, and the store fronts are coming alive with light now, like beckoning potbellied stoves, cherry-hot. There is a calm to the night because autumn is a time of stillness, and even the callous city respects the death of summer. Coat collars are lifted higher, hands are blown upon, hats are tilted lower. The wind is the only sound in the streets, and the citizens walk hastily because they are anxious to get indoors, anxious for the smell of cooking food, and the attacking force of steam heat hissing in radiators, anxious for the arms of loved ones.

Dusk is upon the city.

It will be dark soon.

It will be good to get home before it grows dark.

4.

IN THE DOUGLAS King living room, the telephone rang. King crossed the room quickly, picked up the receiver, and said, 'Hanley?'

A voice on the other end said, 'Who?'

'Oh. Oh, excuse me, I was expecting another call,' King said. 'Who is this, please?'

'All right, Mac,' the voice said. 'I'm going to make this short and—'

There's no one named Mac here,' King said. 'You must have the wrong number.' He replaced the phone and turned toward the steps. Cameron was standing there, watching him.

'Not Hanley?' Cameron said.

'No. Somebody got the wrong number.' King snapped his fingers. 'About wrong numbers, Pete.'

'Yeah?'

'Were you talking to George Benjamin a little while ago?'

'On the phone do you mean?' Cameron asked.

'Yes.'

'As a matter of fact, I was.'

'Why'd you call him?'

'To tell him I wouldn't be around tomorrow. He wanted to discuss that sales letter on the new Far Eastern Brocade line.'

'You didn't tell him you were going to Boston, did you?'

'Why, no. Should I have?'

'Hell, no. What *did* you tell him?'

'Just that I'd have to skip the meeting because I was going out of town.'

'But you didn't mention Boston?'

'Is Boston that important?' Diane asked. 'Can Benjamin smash your deal if he knows where it is?'

'I doubt it. But he'd give his eye teeth to know *who* I'm dealing with – or even that there is a deal cooking. You know, once this thing goes through, I'll be in a position to . . .'

The telephone rang again.

'There it is now,' King said, and he walked quickly to the phone.

'I'd better call for Bobby,' Diane said. 'It's beginning to get dark.'

'Honey, wait until I take this call, will you? I don't want you yelling in the background.' He lifted the receiver. 'Hello?'

'Ready on your call to Boston,' the operator said.

'Okay,' King said.

'Go ahead, sir. Your party is on the line.'

'Hello, Doug?'

'How'd you make out, Hanley?'

'It's all set,' Hanley said wearily. 'I got that five per cent for you.'

'Great! On margin? You got it on margin?'

'Just the way you wanted it, Doug. How soon can you get that cheque up here?'

'I'll send Pete up immediately. Reserve a room for him. Pete, what'd you find out about those planes?'

'Flights leaving Perry Field every hour on the hour.'

'Good.' King looked at his watch. 'Can you make a nine o'clock plane?'

'If you say so,' Cameron said.

'Hanley,' King said into the phone, 'he'll be on the nine o'clock plane. I don't know what time it arrives. You check with the terminal there.'

'Right.'

'And Hanley?'

'Yes, Doug?'

'Good work, boy.' He hung up. 'Now we move!' he said excitedly. 'Pete, call the airline and get that reservation right away!' He snapped his fingers, pushed a button in the face of the phone, lifted the receiver, paused a moment, and then said, 'Reynolds, get over here, will you? On the double.'

'Is everything all set now?' Cameron asked. 'Can you tell me about it now?'

'Now that it's in the bag, I'd even tell Benj – No, no, I guess I wouldn't.' He began chuckling. Quickly he walked to the bar and poured himself a drink.

'I'd better get Bobby,' Diane said. 'Look at how dark it's getting.'

'Let it wait a minute, Diane. Don't you want to hear this?'

'Yes, but—'

'Honey, the boy is in his own back yard, for God's sake.'

'Well . . . all right. But I really . . .'

'You heard Benjamin spouting off, didn't you, Pete? Said that I had thirteen per cent of the voting stock, am I right?'

'Right.'

'Wrong!' King said. He paused, anticipating the dropping of his bombshell. 'I've been buying stock quietly for the past six years. Right now, right this minute, I've got *twenty-eight* per cent of it.'

'Doug, that's wonderful!' Diane said.

'But where does Boston come in?' Cameron asked.

'When did we go up there, Diane? Two weeks ago? Hanley's been there since, lining this up, working on a guy who owns what I call a "disinterested" chunk of voting stock.'

Quickly he crossed to a dropleaf desk in the corner, opened it, and pulled a chequebook toward him. Sitting at the desk, he began filling out the cheque.

'How much of a chunk?' Cameron asked.

'Nineteen per cent.'

'Whaaat!'

'Add it up. Nineteen and twenty-eight make forty-seven. That's enough to swing any election my way, even if those idiots should try to work out something with the Old Man. Enough to make me president of Granger! That means I'll run the company my way, and I'll make whatever damn shoes I want to make!' He ripped the cheque from the book triumphantly and handed it to Cameron. 'Here,' he said, 'take a look at this.'

Cameron took the cheque and emitted a long, low whistle.

'Seven hundred and fifty thousand dollars,' he said, awed.

'And that's on a fifty per cent margin. That stock is costing me a million and a half bucks before this is over and done with. But it's worth it, believe me!'

'Doug, where'd you ever . . . ?'

'I've converted damn near everything we own into cash, Diane. I've even taken a mortgage on this house.'

'A mor—' Diane stared at King speechlessly and then sat, suddenly overwhelmed.

'That's . . . that's a mighty big pile of money,' Cameron said.

'Everything I own! And a tight scrape at that, believe me. I couldn't have got it for a penny less. Diane, this deal is going to make me.'

'I . . . I hope so, Doug.'

'It can't miss, honey. Nobody can stop me now.'

'Who are you buying the stock from, Doug?' Cameron asked.

'A guy who cornered it on the q.t., and who doesn't give a damn how we run the company. He'd just as soon have the cash as—'

'Who?' Cameron said. 'What's his name, Doug?'

'The beautiful part is that he's got the stock spread over about two dozen proxies. Besides us, there isn't a soul who knows he controls such a big chunk.'

'Who? Who is he?' Cameron said.

There was a slight cough at the end of the room. King turned toward the dining room. 'Ah, Reynolds, there you are,' he said. 'I want you to drive Mr Cameron to the airport.'

'What's the rush, Doug?' Cameron said. 'I haven't even got my reservation yet.'

'Well, then get on it right away, will you?'

'And *I'd* better get on Bobby right away,' Diane said. She went to the front door and opened it. 'Bobby!' she called. 'Bobby!'

'We'll have to wait until Mr Cameron makes his

reservation, Reynolds,' King said. 'That shouldn't take too long.'

'Bobby!' Diane called. 'Bob-by!'

The telephone rang. King picked it up.

'Hello?' he said.

'King?'

'Yes, this is Mr King.' He covered the mouthpiece and turned to Pete. 'Come on, Pete, get moving. There isn't much time to lose.'

At the same instant, the voice on the other end said, 'Don't hang up on me this time, King. We're not fooling around here.'

'What? I'm sorry,' King said. 'What did you say?'

'We've got your son, King.'

'My *son*? What are you . . . ?' He turned quickly toward the door.

'Bob-by!' Diane called. 'Bobby, will you *please* answer me?'

'Your son, we've kidnapped your son,' the voice said.

'You . . . you have my son?'

Diane whirled from the open doorway. 'What? What did you say?'

'My . . . my son?' King repeated blankly.

'For the last time, we got your son Bobby. Is that clear?'

'But that's . . . that's impossible.'

'*What is it, Doug?*' Diane shrieked.

'Your son was in the woods, wasn't he?'

'Yes, but— This isn't a joke, is it? If this is a joke . . .'

'This ain't a joke, King.'

'Doug, will you please, please tell me what . . .'

He motioned for her to be silent as the voice on the

phone droned on flatly. 'Now listen and listen hard because I'm only going to say this once. The kid's safe. He'll stay that way as long as you do what we say. We want five hundred thousand dollars in unmarked—'

'Just a minute, I want to take this down.' He reached over for a pencil and pad, snaring them from the desk top, the phone's wire extended to its outermost limits. 'Five hundred thou—'

'In unmarked bills,' the voice said, 'small denominations. You got that?'

'Yes, yes. I've . . . Are you sure you haven't harmed him?'

'He's okay. No consecutive serial numbers on those bills, King. Get the money by tomorrow morning, understand. We'll call you then with further instructions. Don't call the police, King.'

'No. No, I won't.'

'You understand?'

'Yes, dammit. I understand you completely.' Desperately, King's mind searched for a means of trapping the caller. When the idea finally came to him, he executed it swiftly and suddenly, as if he were consummating a long-awaited business deal.

'Okay then,' the voice said, 'five hundred thousand dollars in . . .' and King brought his finger down on the receiver bar, cutting off the connection. He whirled from the phone and shouted, 'Pete, get on the kitchen phone. Call the police first. Tell them Bobby's been kidnapped and we've had a five-hundred-thousand-dollar ransom demand.'

'No!' Diane screamed. '*No!*'

'Then call the phone company. Tell them I hung up on the bastard—'

'Why did you do that? You hung up on the man who has Bobby? You hung up on . . . ?' She could not complete the sentence. She rushed to the front door again and screamed into the gathering darkness, 'Bobby! Bobby! *Bobby!*'

'I hung up on the off chance that he'll call back,' King said. 'The phone company may be able to trace it – and in the meantime, I can think. I can . . .' He paused. 'Reynolds, get my address book upstairs. There's a private detective we used once, when Diane's pearls were missing. Di Bari, something like that, his name is in the book. Call him and get him out here right away.'

'Yes, sir.' Reynolds raced for the steps.

Diane slammed the door and ran to where King stood in the centre of the room. 'Five hundred thousand, you said. All right, call the bank. Right away! Call them this minute, Doug. We've got to get the money to them. We've got to get Bobby back!'

'We will get him back. I'll give them whatever they want, a million if they want it. I'll raise it.' He took Diane into his arms. 'Don't worry, darling. Please, please, try to stop trembling. Try to . . .'

'I'll . . . be all right. It's . . . it's . . .'

Cameron rushed in from the kitchen. 'Police are on their way over, Doug,' he said. 'Phone company standing by. Says to contact them on another line as soon as he calls again.'

'Okay, get in the kitchen. When this phone rings, get the operator to work right away.'

'Right!' Cameron said, and he rushed out of the room again.

Reynolds came down the steps, a defeated expression

on his face. 'I can't find that address book anywhere, sir,' he said. 'I'm sorry. I looked through the telephone table, but . . .'

'I'll get it,' Diane said. With a visible effort, she pulled back her shoulders, moved away from King, and started for the steps. As she passed the front door, it burst open suddenly, startling her.

'Were you calling me, Mom?' Bobby King said.

She blinked her eyes in disbelief. 'Bobby?' she said. And then the name bubbled into her throat with certainty – 'Bobby, Bobby, Bobby!' – and she ran to him and dropped to her knees and pulled him close.

'Hey, what's the matter?' Bobby said.

King looked at his son in puzzlement. 'How . . .' he started, and then he turned toward the phone and pointed a menacing finger at it and shouted, 'Why, that rotten lying . . .'

'I don't want to play with Jeff any more, Mom,' Bobby said. 'I went up a tree like Daddy told me, but it didn't work. I couldn't see him anywhere.'

'What do you mean?' King said and there was sudden fresh alarm in his voice. He glanced at the phone sharply. 'What do you mean, you couldn't see him? Where is he?'

'I'll bet he left the woods,' Bobby said. 'I looked all over, behind every rock. I don't want to play with him any more. He's not anywhere around. I don't know *where* he is!'

There was a moment of stunned silence. The name was on everyone's lips, the truth was in everyone's mind, but it was the boy's father who finally spoke the word, the single word, the name that summed up simply and explicitly everything that had taken place in the woods outside, the name that explained the phone call from a stranger.

'Jeff,' Reynolds said, and the name emerged from his lips as a thin whisper.

In the distance, they could hear a siren coming closer and closer to the cloistered sanctuary that was Smoke Rise.

5.

IF THERE WERE two things that gave Steve Carella the willies, those two things were cases involving extreme wealth and cases involving children. He was not a product of the city's slums and so he couldn't attribute his money willies to a childhood of deprivation. His baker father, Antonio, had always earned a decent living, and Carella had never known the bite of a cold wind on the seat of a pair of threadbare pants. And yet, in the presence of luxury that screamed of wealth, in the drawing rooms and sitting rooms and studies to which his work sometimes took him, Carella felt uneasy. He felt poor. He was not poor, and he'd never been poor, and even if he'd had no money at all he still wouldn't have been poor, but sitting in the Douglas King living room, facing the man who could afford a layout like this one, Steve Carella felt penniless and destitute and somewhat intimidated.

And to top it all off, this looked like a bona fide kidnapping. Even if Carella were not the father of a pair of twins which his wife Teddy had delivered to him this past summer, even if he were not experiencing the first joys of fatherhood, a kidnapping was a damn frightening thing and he wanted no part of it.

Unfortunately, he had no choice.

He sat in the King living room, intimidated, troubled, and he asked his questions while Meyer Meyer looked through the window facing the River Harb, his back to the room.

'Let me get this straight, Mr King,' he said. 'The boy who was kidnapped is *not* your son, is that right?'

'That's right.'

'But the ransom demand was made to you, is that also right?'

'Yes.'

'Then, when the demand was made, the kidnapper thought he was in possession of your son.'

'It would seem so, yes.'

'Were there any further calls?'

'No.'

'Then he may still believe he has your son?'

'I don't know what he believes,' King said angrily. 'Is there really any necessity for all these questions? I am not the boy's father, and I—'

'No, but you're the one who spoke to the kidnapper.'

'That's true.'

'And he asked for five hundred thousand dollars, is that right, Mr King?'

'Yes, yes, yes, Mr Caretta, that's right.'

'Carella.'

'I'm sorry. Carella.'

'This was a man? The person who called.'

'It was a man.'

'When he spoke to you, did he say "*I* have your son" or "*We* have your son"? Would you remember?'

'I don't remember. And I don't see why it's important. *Somebody* has Reynolds' boy, and all this damn semantic—'

'That's exactly it, Mr King,' Carella said. 'Somebody has the boy, and we'd like to find out who that somebody is. You see, we *have* to find out if we're to get that boy back safely. Now that's pretty important to us. Getting the boy back safely, I mean. I'm sure it's just as important to you.'

'Of course it is,' King snapped. 'Why don't you call in the F.B.I., for God's sake? You people aren't equipped to deal with something like this! A boy is kidnapped and . . .'

'Seven days have to elapse before the F.B.I. can enter the case,' Carella said. 'We'll notify them at once, of course, but they can't step in before then. In the meantime, we'll do our best to—'

'Why can't they come in sooner? I thought kidnapping was a Federal offence. Instead of a bunch of local Keystone cops, we could—'

'It's a Federal offence because after seven days have elapsed they can automatically assume a state line has been crossed. Up until that time, it remains in the jurisdiction of the state in which the crime was committed. And in this state, in this city, the local precinct handles the crime. That goes for kidnapping, assault, murder, or what have you.'

'Am I to understand then,' King said, 'that we're going to treat a kidnapping, where a boy's life is in danger, the same way we'd treat a . . . a . . . a fifty-cent item stolen from Woolworth's?'

'Not exactly, Mr King. We've already phoned back to the squad. Lieutenant Byrnes himself is on the way over. As soon as we know a little bit more about—'

'Excuse me, Steve,' Meyer said. 'If we're gonna get a teletype out, I'd better get a description from the boy's father.'

'Yeah,' Carella said. 'Where *is* Mr Reynolds, Mr King?'

'In his apartment. Over the garage. He's taking this pretty badly.'

'Want me to handle it, Meyer?'

'No, no, that's all right.' Meyer glanced significantly at King. 'You seem to have your hands full right here. Where's the garage, Mr King?'

'On the side of the house. You can't miss it.'

'I'll be there if you need me, Steve.'

'Okay,' Carella answered. He turned his attention back to King as Meyer went out of the house. 'Did you notice anything peculiar about this man's voice, Mr King? A lisp, a noticeable accent, a dialect, or . . .'

'I'm sorry, Mr Caretta,' King said, 'but I refuse to play this little game any longer. I honestly don't see what—'

'It's Carella, and what little game were you referring to, Mr King?'

'This cops-and-robbers nonsense. Now what the hell difference could it possibly make whether or not the man lisped or spoke in beautifully cultured English or babbled like a moron? How is that going to get Jeff Reynolds back to his father?'

Carella did not raise his eyes from his notebook. He kept staring at the page upon which he'd been writing, and he kept telling himself it would not seem fitting for a police officer to get up and punch Mr Douglas King in the mouth. Softly, evenly, he said, 'What do you do for a living, Mr King?'

'I run a shoe factory,' King said. 'Is this another one of your very pertinent questions?'

'Yes, Mr King. It is one of my very pertinent

questions. I don't know a thing about shoes, Mr King, except I have to wear them so I won't get tacks in my feet. I wouldn't dream of going into your factory and telling your employees how to nail a sole or glue a heel or sew whatever it is they sew.'

'I get your message,' King said dryly.

'You only get *part* of it, Mr King. You only get the part that's warning you . . .'

'*Warning* me!'

'. . . warning you to cut out what might be misinterpreted as resisting an officer or impeding the progress of an investigation. That's the part you get, and now I'm going to tell you the other part, and I hope both parts penetrate, Mr King, because I'm here to do a job and intend to do it with or without your help. I'm assuming you know how to run a shoe factory or you wouldn't be living here in Smoke Rise with a chauffeur whose son can be mistaken for yours in a kidnapping. Okay. You have no reason to assume I'm a good cop or a bad cop or even an indifferent cop. Most of all, you have no reason to assume I'm a silly cop.'

'I never—'

'To clear up any doubts which may be lingering in your mind, Mr King, I'll tell you now flatly and immodestly that I *am* a good cop, I am a *damn* good cop. I know my job, and I do it well, and any questions I ask you are not asked because I'm auditioning for *Dragnet*. They're all asked with a reason and a purpose, and you'll make things a hell of a lot easier if you answer them without offering any of your opinions on how the investigation should be conducted. Do you think we understand each other, Mr King?'

'I think we understand each other, Mr Caretta.'

'My name is Carella,' Carella said flatly. 'Did the man who called you have any accent?'

Reynolds sat on the edge of the bed, weeping unashamedly, shaking his head over and over again. Meyer watched him, and he bit his lower lip, and he wanted to put his arm around the man's shoulders, comfort him, tell him that everything would be all right. He could not do this because he knew how unpredictable *all* kidnappings were, the boy could be killed before the kidnappers had carried him five miles from the house. And this particular kidnapping had the added danger of error attached to it. How would the louses react when they discovered they had the wrong boy? And so he could not reassure Reynolds, he could only ask the questions he knew by rote, and he could only hope they did not sound absurd to a man who was torn by grief.

'What is the boy's full name, Mr Reynolds?'

'Jeffry. Jeffry.'

'Is that G-e-o-f or J-e-f-f . . . ?'

'What? Oh. J-e-f-f-r-y. Jeffry.'

'Any middle name?'

'No. None.'

'How old is he, Mr Reynolds?'

'Eight.'

'Birth date?'

'September ninth.'

'Then he was just eight, is that right?'

'Yes. Just eight.'

'How tall is he, Mr Reynolds?'

'I . . .' Reynolds paused. 'I don't know. I never . . . I

don't know. Who ever measures children? Who ever expects something like this to . . .'

'Well, approximately, Mr Reynolds? Three feet? Four feet?'

'I don't know. I don't know.'

'Well, average height for that age is somewhere between four and four and a half feet. He's about average height, isn't he, Mr Reynolds?'

'Yes. Or maybe a little tall. He's a handsome boy. Tall for his age.'

'How much does he weigh, Mr Reynolds?'

'I don't know.'

Meyer sighed. 'What about his build? Stout? Medium? Slim?'

'Slender. Not too stout, and not too thin. Just . . . well built for a boy his age.'

'His complexion, Mr Reynolds? Florid, sallow, pale?'

'I don't know.'

'Well, is he a dark kid?'

'No, no. He has blond hair. Very fair skin. Is that what you mean?'

'Yes, thank you. Fair,' Meyer said, and he made a note. 'Hair, blond.' He paused. 'Colour of his eyes, Mr Reynolds?'

'Will you get him back?' Reynolds asked suddenly.

Meyer stopped writing. 'We're going to try,' he said. 'We're going to try our damnedest, Mr Reynolds.'

The description of the boy was phoned in to the 87th and then transmitted to Headquarters, and the teletype alarm went out to fourteen states. The teletype read:

KIDNAP VICTIM JEFFRY REYNOLDS AGE EIGHT HEIGHT APPROX FIFTY-TWO INCHES WEIGHT APPROX

SIXTY POUNDS XXXXXXXX HAIR BLOND EYES BLUE STRAWBERRY BIRTHMARK RIGHT BUTTOCK XXXXXXXX SCAR LEFT ARM CHILDHOOD INJURY FRACTURE XXXXX FATHER'S NAME CHARLES REYNOLDS XXXX MOTHER DECEASED XXXXXX ANSWERS TO NAME JEFF XXXXXX WEARING BRIGHT RED SWEATER BLUE DUNGAREE TROUSERS WHITE SOX SNEAKERS XXXXX NO HAT XXXXX NO GLOVES XXXXX NO JEWELRY XXXXX MAY BE CARRYING TOY RIFLE XXXXX MAY BE IN COMPANY OF MALE XXXXX LAST SEEN VICINITY SMOKE RISE ISOLA SEVENTEEN HUNDRED THIRTY HOURS STD TIME XXXXX STAND BY FOR FURTHER INSTRUCTION ROAD BLOCK COOPERATION XXXXXX CONTACT HQ COMMAND ISOLA ALL INFO ETC XXXXXXXXXX

The message rolled out of teletype machines in police precincts, state trooper command posts, dinky shacks housing local one-horse police forces, anywhere in the surrounding fourteen states where the law enforcement agencies owned and used a teletype machine. It rolled out on a long white sheet with all the monotony of a foreign newspaper. The message immediately following it on the tape read:

REPORTED STOLEN XXX 1949 FORD SEDAN XXXXX EIGHT CYLS XXXX GREY XXXXX ID NUMBER 59 8L 02303 LICENCE PLATE RN 6120 XXXXXX PARKED SUPERMKT PETER SCHWED DRIVE AND LANSING LANE EIGHT HUNDRED HOURS THIS MORNING XXXX CONTACT ONE-OH-TWO PCT RIVERHEAD XXXXX

The grey Ford pulled into the rutted driveway and bounced along the road which had once belonged to a

Sands Spit potato farmer. The road, the land, the farmhouse itself had been sold a long time ago to a man who had purchased the property in the hope that the development boom would reach this isolated neck of the city's suburb. The development boom had come nowhere near reaching the erstwhile potato farm. The speculator, in fact, dropped dead before his dream was realized, and the farm and its adjacent lands, cropless now, run-down, slowly succumbing to the overwhelming encroachment of nature, was handled by a real-estate agent who managed the property for the speculator's daughter, a drunken hag of forty-seven who lived in the city and slept with sailors of all ages. The agent considered it quite a coup when he managed to rent the old farmhouse for a month in the middle of October. Suckers weren't that plentiful in the fall of the year. In the summertime, he could tell prospective tenants that the farm was near the beaches – which it wasn't, being in the centre of Sands Spit and nowhere near either of the peninsula's two shores – and possibly inveigle a city dweller or two into occupying the decrepit wreck for a while. But as soon as Labour Day rolled around, the agent's hopes vanished. The drunken daughter of the speculator would have to find other means of buying her whisky and her sailors. There would be no income from the sagging farmhouse until summer once more returned to Sands Spit. His delight at renting the hulk in the middle of October knew no bounds. Nor did he ever once realize the careful planning that had preceded the rental. He was not a man to look a gift horse in the mouth. Cash was paid on the line. He asked no questions, and expected no answers. Besides, the tenants seemed like a nice young couple. If they wanted to freeze their behinds off in the middle of nowhere, that was their business. His business, like that of the landholders of old, was simply to collect the tithes, man, simply to collect the tithes.

The Ford's headlights probed the blackness of the road, swept the grey farmhouse, the beam swinging around as the car took the curve and then came to a full-braked halt. The engine died. The lights went out. The door on the driver's side opened and a young man in his late twenties stepped into the darkness and ran toward the front door. He knocked gently, three times, and then waited.

'Eddie?' a woman's voice asked.

'It's me, Kathy. Open up.'

The door opened wide. Light splashed onto the frozen earth. The girl looked out into the yard.

'Sy?' she said.

'In the car. He'll be here. Ain't you gonna kiss me?'

'Oh, Eddie, Eddie,' she said, and she threw herself into his arms. She was a woman no older than twenty-four, nor was she a woman who could conceivably be called a 'girl' of twenty-four. For whereas there was a delicate loveliness to her face, the beauty had been overlaid with a veneer of hardness, the look of shellac worn thin, marred by years of use and misuse. Kathy Folsom was a *woman* of twenty-four and perhaps, perhaps she had even been a woman of twelve at one time. She wore a straight black skirt and a blue sweater, the sleeves shoved up to her elbows. Her hair was obviously bleached, showing dark at the roots and at the part, but on Kathy it somehow did not appear cheap, it only seemed untended, uncared for. She held her husband to her with a desperation that had been mounting ever since he had left the farmhouse that afternoon. She kissed him longingly, her arms wrapped around his waist, and then she drew away from him and stared up into his face, and she smiled with a tenderness that was embarrassing even to herself, and then, to cover her embarrassment, she touched his cheek quickly and said again, 'Eddie, Eddie,' and then, sharply, 'Are you all right? Did everything go all right?'

'Everything went fine,' Eddie said. 'How about here? Any troubles?'

'No, none. I was sitting on pins and needles. I kept thinking, This is the last one; please, God, don't let anything go wrong.'

'Well everything went just the way we figured it.' He paused. 'You got a cigarette, honey?'

'In my bag. On the chair there.'

He crossed to the chair quickly and rummaged in her purse. She watched him as he lighted the cigarette, a tall good-looking man wearing dark slacks and sports jacket, a white shirt open at the throat, a maroon sweater over the shirt.

'I was listening to the radio,' Kathy said. 'I thought they might mention something. I mean, after all, a bank and all.' She paused. 'It went all right, didn't it? There was no trouble?'

'No trouble.' He blew out a stream of smoke. 'Only, Kathy, you see . . . well . . . we didn't exactly . . .'

She kissed him again, swiftly, as if unable to keep her lips from his a moment longer. 'You're back,' she whispered. 'That's all that matters.'

'In here, kid,' the voice said, and there was a push in the voice, and a physical push in the hands of the man owning the voice. Jeff Reynolds stumbled into the room, and the man behind him chuckled and then slammed the door behind him, and then said, 'Ah, home again! How do you like it, kid? It ain't much, but it reeks, don't it?' He chuckled again. His laugh seemed to match his appearance. He was forty-two years old, nattily dressed in a dark suit, though badly in need of a shave. There was a curious air about him, the air of a man who is enjoying himself at the firm's annual picnic.

'Where's my gun?' Jeff said, and Kathy turned at the sound of his voice and then looked at him in bewilderment. He did not seem at all frightened, a little wide-eyed perhaps, slightly upset by the strange surroundings, but otherwise content.

'The boy wants his gun,' Sy said, smiling. 'Where's the gun we promised him?'

Kathy kept staring at Jeff. 'Who . . . who the hell . . . ?' she started, and Sy's grin expanded into a chuckle and then a gust of exuberant laughter.

'Ahhhh, look, Eddie, look at that beautiful piece of surprise on her face. Oh, man, this tickles me!'

'Let me handle this, Sy,' Eddie said.

'Where's the gun?' Jeff said. 'Come on, I have to be getting back.' He turned to Kathy. 'Have *you* got the gun?'

'Wh-what gun?' she answered automatically, and then she shouted, 'Who is this kid? Where . . . ?'

'Who is he?' Sy said, grinning. 'What a question to ask. Where's your manners, doll? We bring a guest home, and right away you get personal.'

She whirled on her husband instantly. 'Eddie, who . . . ?'

'Permit me, please,' Sy said, bowing from the waist. 'Son, this is Kathy Folsom, née Kathy Neal, pride of the

South Side. Beautiful, ain't she? Feast your eyes. Kathy, this is King—' he paused, reaching, and then said '—of the wild frontier!' exploding into a fresh gale of laughter, convulsed by his own humour.

'What's he talking about, Eddie? Where'd you get this boy? What's he doing here? Why . . . ?'

'I'll bet you haven't got a gun at all,' Jeff said.

'We ain't, huh?' Sy answered, 'Kid, we got enough artillery here to start a second Civil War. If General Lee had himself so many guns, we'd be asking your old man for *Confederate* bills right now.' He laughed again, a laugh of defiance which he tossed at Kathy as if challenging her intelligence. The challenge was unnecessary. The reference to bills had not escaped her. The meaning was instantly and shockingly clear. She turned to her husband and said, 'Eddie, you haven't . . .'

'Come on, kid,' Sy said. 'Let's get that gun.' He shoved Jeff to the door leading from the large parlour-kitchen of the farmhouse to one of the bedrooms. 'The gun and trophy room is right this way,' he said. 'All the comforts of home, huh?'

She waited until the door closed behind them. Then she said to Eddie, 'All right, tell me about it.'

'It's what it looks like,' Eddie said. His voice was low. He would not raise his eyes to meet hers.

'Have you lost your mind?' she asked. 'Have you gone completely out of your mind?'

'Relax now, will you? Just try to relax a little.'

Trembling to maintain control, Kathy walked stiffly to her purse, opened it, shook free a cigarette, which fell instantly from her fingers, managed to keep one in her hand while she lighted it, and then said, 'All right. I'm listening.'

'It's a snatch,' Eddie said simply.

'Why?'

'Whatya mean, why? There's five hundred grand involved here.'

'You said . . .'

'Do you need more reason than that? For Christ's sake, this is—'

'You said a bank. That was bad enough, but at least . . .'

'I was lying. It never was a bank. I only said that. We didn't go anywhere near a bank.'

'No, I see you didn't. Don't you know how serious this is, Eddie? Kidnapping is a Federal offence! You can get the electric chair for this!'

'Only if the kid ain't returned before the case goes to trial.'

'You're already in the courtroom and this is the first I'm even *hearing* of it! How long have you been planning this thing?'

'About . . . about six months now.'

'Whaaat?'

'Now look, calm down. There's no sense getting excited.'

'Who is he?'

'Bobby King.'

'And who's Bobby King?'

'His old man is a big wheel in Granger Shoe. You know the company, hon. They put out these expensive shoes for dames.'

'Yes, I know the company.' She was silent for a moment. Then, very softly, she said, 'Why didn't you tell me what you were planning?'

'Well, I didn't think you'd go along with it. I figured . . .'

'Damn right I won't go along with it!' Kathy shouted. 'Get that boy out of here this minute! Take him back where you got him!'

'How can we do that?' Eddie said. 'Come on, be sensible, will you?'

'If you don't take him back, *I* will.'

'Yeah, sure.'

'His parents must be going crazy by now. How could you do a thing—'

'Now shut up a minute, will you?' Eddie said harshly. 'He's staying right here until we get the loot, so that's that, so just shut up.'

Kathy walked to an ash tray and stubbed out her cigarette. She went to the window then and stared out at the front yard.

Eddie watched her. Gently, he said, 'Kathy?'

'You told me to shut up, didn't you?'

'Honey, there's five hundred grand in this,' he said plaintively. 'Can't you . . .'

'I don't want it.'

'Half for us, half for Sy.'

'Not any part of it! I wouldn't touch it!'

'It'll take us to Mexico.'

The hell with you and Mexico!'

'I don't understand you,' Eddie said, shaking his head. 'You said you *wanted* to go to Mexico.'

'And you said this was the last time,' she shouted, whirling from the window. The last one, you said, that's what *you* said. A bank. A simple bank. Just to set us up in—'

'All right!' Eddie said triumphantly. 'All right, it *is*

the last one. Now how about that? Five hundred thousand dollars! An express train right to Acapulco!'

'On a kidnapping! Couldn't you think of a filthier, more rotten . . .'

'A kidnapping, so what? Did we hurt the kid? Did we touch him? He's fine, ain't he?'

Remembering the boy, Kathy turned toward the bedroom door. 'What's Sy doing to him in there?' she said, and she began walking toward the door instantly.

Eddie caught her arm. 'He's all right. Sy promised him a real gun. That's how we got him here. Look honey, try to understand this, will you?'

'I don't want to understand anything about it. Dammit, don't you draw the line anyplace? What *gave* you this crazy idea to begin with? What the hell possibly gave you . . . ?'

'I just got it, that's all. We worked it out.'

'*Who* worked it out? You?' She paused. 'Or Sy?'

'We worked it out together.' He studied her face for a moment and then said, 'Well, look, what's the sense risking our necks on a stickup, huh? This is safer, ain't it? We borrow a kid, and when we return him we get five hundred grand. Now ain't that safer?'

'Borrow? Who said that? Sy?'

'No, no, for Pete's sake, I told you we worked this out together.'

'Did you, Eddie?'

'Yes. Yes.'

'You're lying, Eddie. It was Sy's idea, wasn't it?'

Well . . .'

Wasn't it?'

'Well, it was.' Then hastily, he said, 'But it's a good idea, Kathy, can't you see that? We can really quit after this one, I mean it, honey. Now look, honey, I mean it – this is the last one. Look, I can . . . I can maybe really get to be something in Mexico. Hey now, wouldn't that be great, huh? Eddie Folsom, huh? Me. Something, you know?'

'Eddie, Eddie,' she said, 'don't you even realize what you've done?'

'Honey, look, believe me, this is gonna be all right. I promise you, Kathy. Now, have I ever let you down, huh? Just stick with me, honey, willya? Please?'

She did not answer.

'Honey?'

She still did not answer.

'Aw, honey, please try to . . .'

'Bang!' Jeff shouted, and he ran into the room carrying a shotgun, Sy grinning behind him. 'Wow, what a gun!'

'The kid likes guns,' Sy said, laughing. 'Play with the gun, kid. Get to know it.'

'Sy, is that loaded?' Kathy said, alarmed.

'Now would I give a loaded gun to a mere child?' Sy asked. He clucked his tongue in imitation of an old lady.

'It sure *is* loaded, lady,' Jeff said. He aimed the gun and yelled, 'Bang! Right between the eyes!'

'Okay, kid, knock it off,' Sy said. 'Slow down a little.' He frowned momentarily and then said, 'How about tuning in the monster, Eddie?'

Eddie looked at Kathy helplessly, as if begging her with his eyes to understand. But she would not understand, and he read that on her face, and despondently he said, 'Sure, Sy,' and walked to the far wall of the parlour and immediately pulled a tarpaulin covering from a mass of radio equipment which was stacked against the wall.

'Kid,' Sy said to Jeff, 'this is Dr Frankenstein. Watch him bring that monster to life.'

The equipment did not, in truth, resemble a monster. There was however, some validity to Sy's allusion, in that the dials and switches, the needles and knobs would not have seemed inappropriate in a scientist's laboratory. Eddie walked to the setup and threw a switch.

'Go ahead, show off for the kid,' Sy said. 'Tell him what frequency the police calls are on.'

Absorbed with tuning the receiver, Eddie replied, 'Thirty-seven point fourteen megacycles.'

'Oh, the brain on that doctor,' Sy said. 'Kathy, you hooked yourself a prize, a real prize.'

'Why'd you drag my husband into this?' Kathy said tightly. 'Why didn't you leave him alone?'

'Drag? Who, me? He come in willingly, sweetheart.' A high piercing shriek erupted from the receiver. 'There she goes, kid,' Sy said. 'The monster's beginnin' to speak.'

'Hey, that's really something,' Jeff said. 'Where'd you get it?'

'I built it,' Eddie answered.

'No kidding? Boy, that musta been hard.'

'Well, it . . .' Struggling with his pleasure, reluctant to sound too proud, Eddie said, 'It wasn't *too* hard.'

'Nothing's hard for a mastermind, huh, Kathy?' Sy said. 'You're a real electronic wizard, ain't you, Eddie? That's why the little woman loves you. Learned it all in reform school, too, didn't you?'

'Cut it out,' Kathy said.

'What's the matter? I'm complimenting your husband. Someday, kid, Eddie's gonna go to a real school, be a regular schoolboy and learn radio inside out and backwards. Ain't that right, Eddie. Tell the kid here.'

Embarrassed, Eddie said, 'Yeah, that's right.'

'Thomas Alva Frankenstein, that's who he is, sonny. You want to learn how to build a set like that and have all the dames fall for you, kid?'

'I'll say I do!' Jeff said.

'Okay, then here's how. When you're fifteen years old, hold up a grocery store.'

'Sy, what are you telling him?' Kathy snapped.

'What's the matter?' Sy asked innocently. 'You don't even need a gun, kid. Just stick your hand in your pocket like Eddie did. When they catch you, they'll send you over to Youth House, and then to Children's Court, and then to reform school. Am I right, Eddie?'

More embarrassed now, twisting the radio dial intently, Eddie said, 'Yeah, that's right. Sure.'

'In reform school,' Sy concluded, 'they'll teach you how to make radios. Am I right, Eddie?'

'Only how to fix them.'

'I don't see anything funny about this, Sy,' Kathy said.

'Who's being funny? I'm teaching the kid a trade. Shall I tell him all the other things you learned in reform school, Eddie? The other *trades*?'

'Aw, tell him whatever the hell you want to.'

'Now, now, watch your language in front of the boy,' Sy said. He grinned and tousled Jeff's hair. 'Me, kid, all I ever learned was how to work in the jute mill. You ever work with jute? Don't. It makes you sneeze. It crawls into your lungs. It even crawls up your asshole.' Sy began laughing. 'How's it coming, Doctor?'

'I'm getting it,' Eddie said, and the radio suddenly erupted into intelligible sound.

'. . . thirteen. Accident at Morrison and North Ninety-eight. Car 303, signal thirteen. Accident at Morrison and North Ninety-eight.'

'This is 303. Okay.'

'A snatch right under their noses,' Sy said, 'and they're worried about a traffic jam.'

'Hey, you going to take me back now?' Jeff asked.

'I'm busy, kid.'

Jeff turned to Kathy. 'How about you?' He studied her for a moment, frankly, candidly. Then, having formed his opinion, he said, 'Aw, you're a girl. What can girls do?'

Sy burst out laughing. 'Kid,' he said, 'you'd be surprised.'

'*Car 207, Car 207,*' the police dispatcher said. '*Signal thirteen, join and assist Car 204 at Douglas King estate, Smoke Rise, adjacent River Highway on Smoke Rise Road. Signal thirteen, join and assist . . .*'

'Hey, did you hear that?' Jeff said, excited by his discovery. 'He said Douglas King!'

'*. . . Smoke Rise, adjacent River Highway on Smoke Rise Road.*'

'This is 207. Right.'

'The long arm of the law is beginning to reach,' Sy said. 'What'd I tell you? Ask those crumbs not to call the cops, and it's the first thing they do.' He shook his head sadly. 'You can't trust nobody nowadays.'

'Do you really expect to get away with this, Sy?' Kathy asked.

'Why, certainly. And all because Dr Frankenstein has ideas. Me, I got a worthless hobby. Swing music. Can swing music help us on a thing like this? Can Harry James blow his way out of this one? Ahhh, but Eddie's hobby, a dream, a dream. Radios.' He closed his thumb against his fingers and then kissed the collective bunch. 'I love them. I love radios. I love Eddie.' He paused. 'I even love you, Kathy. Outline it for her, Doctor.'

'She doesn't want to hear it,' Eddie said.

'She don't?' Sy said, surprised. 'What's the matter, baby, you coldhearted or something? This gig's gonna go down in history, believe me. And all because Eddie knows radio. Right now, we're listening to the bulls on his monster there. But later . . . Man, when I think of this scheme, it gives me goose bumps.'

'Sy, she's not interested,' Eddie said.

'I'm interested in anything you do,' Kathy said softly.

'Why, sure she is. The little woman. Okay,' Sy said, 'we called King on the way here. Told him we wanted five hundred grand, told him to get it ready by—'

Jeff blinked. 'Did you say you called . . . ?'

'Shut up, kid. Told him to get it ready by tomorrow morning, and we'd call him then to let him know where and when the drop's gonna be. Now here's the beauty part, honey. You listening?'

'I'm listening.'

'Okay. Tomorrow morning, we buzz King again. We tell him—'

'Are you talking about—' Jeff started, and Sy shouted, 'I said shut up, kid, now take a goddamn hint!' He glared at Jeff heatedly.

Jeff put his hands on his hips, swaggered over to Sy and, entering into the game, using his best tough-guy voice, said, 'Who do you think you are, Mac?'

'Blow kid, before you get hurt.'

Still playing, Jeff said, 'You want to get tough with me, mister?'

'I said blow!' Sy shoved the boy aside angrily. Jeff, startled, stared at him and then frowned. The room was silent. And then piercing the silence, the radio came to life again.

'Attention all cars, attention all cars. Here's the story on that Smoke Rise kidnapping.'

'Hey, listen,' Eddie said.

'Be on the lookout for a blond, eight-year-old boy wearing bright-red sweater, blue dungaree trousers, white socks and sneakers, no hat, no gloves, may be carrying a toy rifle.'

'You're famous, kid,' Sy said, grinning.

'The boy's name is Jeffry Reynolds, answers to the name Jeff . . . '

'What?' Eddie said.

'That man said my name,' Jeff said, startled.

'Shut up!' Sy snapped.

'. . . is the son of Charles Reynolds, chauffeur on the King estate. There's been some kind of a foul-up here, boys, and your guess is as good as mine. There's been a five-hundred-thousand-dollar ransom demand, so chances are the kidnappers don't know who they've got yet. Beats me. Anyway, that's the story, and that's all.'

'What's he talking about, Sy?' Eddie said. Panic had covered his face like a coat of white paint. He stared at Sy, his eyes demanding an answer, his entire body demanding an answer.

'That man said my name,' Jeff said, astonished.

'They're lying,' Sy said quickly. 'They're trying to put one over on us.'

'On police radio, Sy? They don't even know we're listening!'

'No, all they know is they want to get us, so they're pulling a cheap trick. And don't think King ain't in on this. That crooked bastard!'

'How could we have grabbed the wrong kid?' Eddie wailed.

'He *ain't* the wrong kid!'

'But suppose he is?' Kathy said calmly. 'It means you've done all this for nothing. We're in trouble for nothing.'

Eddie looked at his wife, and then at Sy. 'You . . . you gonna believe what the cops tell you?' he said. 'Kathy, you can't believe *them*!'

'Who can you believe? Sy?'

'Why not?' Sy said. 'I say this kid is Bobby King. Now how about that?'

'Me?' Jeff said, puzzled. 'I'm not Bobby.'

'One more peep out of you—'

'Let him talk,' Kathy said. 'What's your name, sonny?'

'Jeff.'

'He's lying!' Sy shouted.

'I am not!' Jeff shouted back. He glared at Sy and then said, 'I don't like you, you know that? I'm going home.'

He started for the door. Sy caught his arm and yanked him back, almost pulling him off his feet. He stood very close to the boy, and there was no humour on his face now, no laughter in his eyes. In a flat, emotionless voice he said, 'What's your name? Your *real* name.'

6.

THE DRIVEWAY TO the King estate was flanked by two stone pillars, each of which carried an ornate glass-and-wrought-iron lantern. The pillars were set back some three feet from the private Smoke Rise Road which ran past the estate, the communications link between Smoke Rise and the outside world. Between the pillars and the gravel road was a shelf of grass. Grass, in fact, lined both sides of the road, framing the grey ribbon with an October-bitten off-green.

The road was generally barren, especially on nights like this one when October was trying its best to serve as a harbinger of dead winter. A cold wind had come up, blowing off the River Harb, sending everyone but mad dogs, Englishmen, and policemen indoors. There was, perhaps, a slight difference in the motivation of the triumvirate. For whereas mad dogs stayed outside because of the vagaries of insanity, and Englishmen because of their internationally renowned *sang-froid*, the policemen were there under duress. There was not a policeman on that road that night who would not have preferred being at home with a good book, or a good woman, or a good bottle of brandy. There was not a policeman present that night who would not have preferred even a bad book or a bad bottle of brandy or, to be frankly unpatriotic, a bad woman.

There were no women, good or bad, on that road that night.

There were only men, and men engrossed in their work can be dull company to each other even when the weather is mild.

'I never seen it so cold in October in my whole life,' Detective Andy Parker said. 'I been living in this city my whole life, and I never seen it so cold like this. Tonight, they better bring in the brass monkeys, I am telling you. Tonight, everything freezes.'

Detective Cotton Hawes nodded. His fingers around the flashlight, even through the leather, fur-lined gloves he wore, felt frozen to the bone. He kept the circle of light on the patch of grass across the road from the driveway pillars. The lab technician at his feet, a man named Peter Kronig, was a person with whom Hawes had had a slight brush not too long ago. Hawes could not say now whether or not he disliked holding the light for Kronig while Kronig searched the grass on his hands and knees. He knew that he'd ridden Kronig's tail pretty shamefully on their one previous encounter, and he was rather embarrassed by their proximity now. Of course, Hawes had been working at the 87th Precinct for only a short time when he had first run across Kronig. Like any new kid on the block, he was anxious to prove himself to the other kids. In the presence of Steve Carella, whom he immediately considered the best cop on the squad, Hawes had begun riding Kronig at the police lab. Carella had chewed him out later, in a kindly fashion to be sure, and Hawes had learned a valuable lesson: Don't make enemies of the lab technicians. He had learned his lesson well. Its meaning assumed renewed importance now that he was once more working with Kronig.

'Move the light,' Kronig said. 'Over to the left.'

Hawes moved the light.

'It's only sixteen degrees,' Parker said. 'Can you feature that? It feels like twenty below, don't it? But it's only sixteen. I heard it over the radio. Man, it's cold. Ain't it cold, Hawes?'

'Yes,' Hawes answered.

'You don't talk much, do you?'

'I talk,' Hawes said. He did not particularly feel like justifying himself to Andy Parker. He didn't know the man too well, this being the first time they'd been on a squeal together, but from what he'd seen of him around the squadroom, Parker was a man it paid to stay away from. At the same time, Hawes did not want to make the same mistake he'd made with Kronig. He did not want to make an enemy where he could make a friend. 'It's just that my teeth are frozen together,' he added, hoping this would mollify Parker.

Parker nodded. He was a big man, almost as tall as Hawes, who stood six feet two inches high in his bare soles. But whereas Hawes's eyes were blue and his hair was red (except for a white streak over the left temple), Parker gave an impression of darkness, black hair, brown eyes, five o'clock shadow. And, in all honesty, the two men could not have been more dissimilar than their appearances indicated. Hawes was a cop who was still learning. Parker was a cop who knew it all.

'Hey, Kronig,' he said, 'what the hell are you searching for? Buried treasure? We got nothing better to do than crawl around on our hands and knees?'

'Shut up, Parker,' Kronig answered. 'I'm the one

who's doing the crawling. All you're doing is bitching about the weather.'

'What, you ain't cold?' Parker said. 'You got Eskimo blood?' He paused. 'Eskimos lend out their wives, you know that?'

'I know,' Kronig said. 'Let's try over here, Hawes. Come on.'

They moved several feet up the road, the flashlight playing on the grassy shoulder lining the gravel.

'It's the truth,' Parker said, 'whether you know it or not. An Eskimo goes to visit another Eskimo, he lets you borrow his wife for the night. So you shouldn't get cold.' Parker shook his head. 'And they call *us* civilized. Would you lend me your wife for the night, Kronig?'

'I wouldn't lend you a nickel for a cup of coffee,' Kronig answered. 'Over here, Hawes. This looks like something.' He stooped suddenly.

'I didn't ask for a nickel, I asked for your wife,' Parker said, and he grinned in the darkness. 'You should see this guy's wife, Hawes. Like a movie star. Am I right, Kronig?'

'Go blow it out,' Kronig answered. 'It's nothing, Hawes. Let's move up a little.'

'What are you looking for?' Hawes asked, as gently as he knew how.

Kronig stared at him for a moment, his breath pluming from his mouth. 'Footprints, tyre tracks, traces of clothing, matches, any damn thing that might give us a lead.'

'Well,' Hawes said gently, 'I don't want to stick my two cents in. You know your job, and I have no right to offer any suggestions.'

'Yeah?' Kronig said. He looked at him suspiciously.

'Seems to me the last time we met, you had a lot of suggestions, and a lot of answers. You knew all about ballistics, didn't you? The Annie Boone case, wasn't it?'

'That's right,' Hawes said.

'Yeah, so now you're shy, huh? The shy flower of the Eighty-seventh Squad.'

'I've got no quarrel with you,' Hawes said. 'I behaved like a jerk that time.'

'Yeah?' Kronig said, surprised. He kept staring at Hawes. Then he said, 'What's your suggestion? I'm not God.'

'Neither am I. But would the kidnapper be likely to park the car here, or to stand here, or to do anything here where he could be seen? I mean, right on the road?'

'Possibly not. Where do you think he parked?'

'There's a turnabout up there. About five hundred yards from the pillars. Just a little dirt cutoff. It's pretty well screened with bushes. It's worth a chance.'

'Then let's try it,' Kronig said.

'Like a movie star,' Parker said. 'This guy's wife. She's got knockers out to here. You never seen knockers like on this guy's wife except on the silver screen. Man, I'm telling you!'

'Shut up, Parker,' Kronig said.

'I'm complimenting your wife. It ain't everybody got breastworks like this woman got. Man, you could lose yourself up there. You could bury your nose, and your mouth, and your whole goddamn head if you—'

'Shut up, Parker!' Kronig said. 'I don't feel like discussing my wife's attributes with you, if you don't mind.'

'What are you?' Parker asked. 'The nervous type?'

'Yeah, I'm the nervous type.'

'And they call the Eskimos primitive,' Parker said. 'Man!'

The men trudged up the gravel road silently. The night was a piece of crystal, sharp, clear, brittle. Like work horses stamping under a heavy load, they walked to the turnabout, the vaporized moisture of their breath trailing behind them.

'This it?' Kronig asked.

'Yes,' Hawes said. 'I noticed it when we drove up.'

'Not a very big turnabout, if that's what it is.' He shook his head. 'I don't think it's a turnabout at all. Or at least I don't think it was planned as one. I think it just *became* one through use. There. See where some of those shrubs were knocked over?'

'Yeah,' Hawes said. 'But a car could have waited here, don't you think?'

'Sure, it could have. Let's have some light on the subject.'

Hawes turned on the flash. The beam covered the ground.

'Frozen mud,' Parker said disgustedly. 'Like Italy during the war. More than fifteen years go by, and I'm still up to my ass in frozen mud.'

'Any tracks?' Hawes asked.

'Anything I hated,' Parker said, 'it was trudging through the mud. You walk around in that slime all day long, and then you sleep in it all night long and next day you get up and walk around in it some more. And cold? You touched the barrel of your BAR and your hand stuck to it, that's how cold it was.'

'You should have joined the Navy,' Kronig said drily. 'I think we've got something here, Hawes.'

'What is it?'

'A skid mark. Somebody pulled out of here in a hell of a hurry.'

'That figures.' Hawes knelt beside Kronig. 'Does it look any good?'

'It's covered with a thin sheet of ice.' Kronig nodded reflectively, as if he were suddenly alone. 'Well, let's see what we can do with it, huh?'

He opened his black bag and Hawes brought the flash up so that he could see into it.

'Shellac,' Kronig said, 'sprayer, talcum, plaster, water, rubber cap, spoon and spatula. I'm in business. There's only one thing I'd like to know.'

'What's that?' Hawes said.

'Do I spray my shellac over the ice, or do I try to get rid of the ice with the possibility of damaging the tyre pattern?'

'That's a good question,' Hawes said.

'One thing you sure as hell can't do,' Parker said, 'and that's wait for the ice to melt. Winter's here to stay.'

'Andy Parker, boy optimist,' Kronig said. 'Why don't you take a walk or something?'

That's just what I'm going to do,' Parker said. 'Back to the house where I can get a cup of coffee from the cook. She's got knockers almost as big as your wife's.'

The man from the telephone company drilled another hole in the woodwork, handed the drill to Reynolds, and then blew the sawdust out of the hole. Squatting close to the floor, he eyed the hole like a cat waiting for a mouse, and then stood up.

'Okay,' he said. 'Now for the wire.' He started across

the room, passing Carella, who was busy on the telephone.

'You got nothin' to worry about, mister,' the telephone company man said to Reynolds. 'Figure it out for yourself. When they find out they got your kid by mistake, they'll just turn him loose, it figures, don't it?'

'It just seems we should have heard something by now,' Reynolds said.

'Look, don't get nervous,' the man said. 'You start gettin' nervous, you lost half the battle, it figures, don't it?'

On the phone, Carella said, 'Well, what the hell's the holdup there? Are you getting me a line to the Auto Squad, or aren't you?' He paused. 'Then would you please get the lead out of your behind? A kid's been kidnapped here!'

'Do you have any children, Mr Cassidy?' Reynolds asked the telephone company man.

'I got four,' Cassidy said. 'Two of each. That's a nice family, ain't it?'

'Very nice.'

'I'm thinking of maybe another one, round it off, that figures, don't it? Five's a good round number, I told the wife.' He paused. 'She said four is a round-enough number.' He picked up a spool of wire and began paying it out across the living-room floor. 'That's the trouble with women nowadays. You want to know something?'

'What?'

'In China, the women have their babies in the rice fields, it figures, don't it? They drop their ploughs, and they deliver the kids themselves, and then they get right up off the ground and go back to ploughing or whatever it is they do with rice. It figures, don't it?'

'Well, I don't know,' Reynolds said. 'What's the mortality rate?'

'Gee, I don't know what the mortality rate is,' Cassidy said. He paused thoughtfully. Then he said, 'But I *do* know very few of them die.' He paused again. 'It figures, don't it?'

'If they'd turned him loose,' Reynolds said, 'wouldn't someone have seen him already?'

'Mister, I told you not to start worryin', didn't I? Okay, so stop. Now that kid's all right, you hear me? For God's sake, he's the wrong kid. What can they do to him – *kill* him?'

'Well, it's about time,' Carella said into the phone. 'What's going on down there, a hot pinochle game?' He listened for a moment, and then said, 'This is Steve Carella of the Eighty-seventh. I'm up in Smoke Rise on this kidnapping. We thought – What do you mean, *what* kidnapping? Are you in the Police Department or the Department of Sanitation? It's only on every radio in the city.'

'If they turn him loose in the street,' Reynolds said, 'he won't know where to go. He isn't the kind of child who can find his way around easily.'

'Mister, *any* kid can find his way around, it figures, don't it?'

'Anyway,' Carella said into the phone, 'we thought we'd run a check on stolen cars just in case the car used in the snatch was—' He paused. 'What? Listen, mister, what's your name? . . . Okay, Detective Planier, I've already heard all the jokes about snatches, and I don't think they're very funny right now. What do you do when a guy turns up dead in a pine coffin, crack jokes about boxes? There's an eight-year-old kid missing here, and we want a rundown on stolen cars, so get a list up here right away . . . . What? . . . No, just covering the last week or ten days. Thank you, Detective Planier. . . . What? Up your mother's too,' Carella said. 'The address is just Douglas King, Smoke Rise. Off Smoke Rise Road. Goodbye, Detective Planier.' He hung up and turned to Cassidy. 'Wise guy,' he said. 'I broke up a pinochle game.'

'Did they have any news, Detective Carella?' Reynolds asked.

'I was only talking to Auto Squad,' Carella answered.

'Oh.'

'He's all worried,' Cassidy said. 'I keep tellin' him there's nothing to worry about. In fact, even puttin' in this extra phone is a waste of time. The kid'll be back before you can say Jack Robinson, it figures, don't it?'

'Do *you* think so?' Reynolds asked Carella.

'Well . . .' Carella answered, and the doorbell rang. He rose from the phone table and went to answer it. Parker came into the room, slapping his arms against his sides.

'Whoooo!' he said. 'The North Pole!'

'Cold out there?'

'Whoooo!' Parker said again. 'How's it going in here? Nice and warm in here, Stevie? You should be outside with the mad scientist.'

'What's Kronig doing?'

'Trying to make a cast from a tyre track. After that, he'll probably dust the whole damn driveway for fingerprints. These lab boys give me a fat pain in the keester. Goddamn mad scientists. The kid's probably dead already, anyway.' Carella gave him a sharp poke in the ribs. 'What's the matter?' Parker asked.

Carella glanced hastily toward Reynolds, who had apparently not heard Parker's remark. 'Any sign of the lieutenant yet?' he asked.

'No, I ain't seen him. He's probably curled up home with his wife.' He studied Cassidy, who was trailing his length of coloured wires across the room. 'What the hell is *he* doing?'

'Putting in a trunk line to the phone company's main office.'

'And what's that?' Parker asked, pointing to the instrument set up near the telephone.

'You know damn well what that is. It's a wiretap.'

'All baloney,' Parker said. 'Wiretap, trunk line, all baloney! I never seen such a commotion in my life. I won't be surprised we get the Chief of Detectives in here.'

'I imagine the lieutenant will call him,' Carella said.

'Sure, and for what? The lab's outside crawling around on their hands and knees sniffing tyre tracks, and the whole damn force is out checking rooming houses and hotels and motels and every fleabag in the city and the suburbs. We got dicks at both airports and covering every train station, bus terminal and trolley car stop. And I ask you, for what? Those cheap thieves got only two choices open to them.'

'Have they, Andy?'

'Damn right. They either turn the kid loose or they kill him out of spite.'

'They ought to take all kidnappers and burn them at the stake,' Cassidy said. 'Man sweats his head off raising a nice family, and some guy steps in and swipes a kid. There ought to be a law.'

'You . . . you don't think they'll . . . harm Jeff, do you, Detective Carella?' Reynolds asked. 'When they find out he isn't the one they wanted?'

'There ain't nobody safe nowadays, nobody,' Cassidy said. 'That's because the cops are all a bunch of—' He stopped suddenly, seemingly realizing that he was in the presence of policemen. Casually, he cleared his throat. 'Maybe I better test this phone, huh?' he said. He picked up the receiver of the new phone. Impatiently, he jiggled the bar. 'Hello? Hello?'

'I'm going to the kitchen for a cup of coffee,' Parker said. 'You want some, Stevie?'

'No. Thanks.'

'Wiretaps, trunk lines,' Parker said disgustedly, and he walked out of the room.

'Hello,' Cassidy said into the telephone, 'this is Cassidy . . . . What? . . . Never mind the Hopalong wisecracks. I'm testing this Smoke Rise installation.' He listened. 'Yeah . . . . Okay. Fine. I'm finished, then. What else you got for me?' He listened, jotting an address on to a pad. 'Right. So long.' He hung up. 'Well, that does it.'

'All finished?'

'Just pick it up, and you've got our main office. You going to try tracing a call, huh?'

'If we get another call to trace.'

'I'll let you in on something, Officer. But don't spread it around. If your man uses a dial phone, you ain't got a chance in hell of tracing the call. You know?'

'I know,' Carella said.

'Oh. You know. Well, you better pray he uses a

manual instrument. That sounds like a dirty joke, hey, don't it?' He chuckled to himself, took some papers from his pocket and then glanced at his watch. 'Are them three gonna be eating dinner all night? I gotta get somebody to sign for this installation.'

'They should be finished soon,' Carella said.

'You never seen an outfit like this one for getting things signed,' Cassidy said. 'You want to go to the toilet, you got to get somebody to sign for it, it figures, don't it?' He shook his head. 'I swear to God, one of these days, the telephone company is gonna declare war on the United States.'

'Have you heard anything yet, Detective Carella?' King said, and he came through the dining-room arch and into the living room, carrying a coffee cup in his right hand. Diane and Cameron were directly behind him.

'Not yet, Mr King,' Carella said.

'Mr King, I wonder if you would si—' Cassidy started.

'Well, what's the holdup?' King said. 'Are you sure your men are really looking? Do they have a description of the boy?'

'Yes, sir, they have a description.'

'Would you sign this—'

'Do they know he'll be wandering the streets? They can't expect the kidnappers to deliver him to our front—'

'Yes, sir, they know that.'

'Could you sign this form we—'

'Well, then, why hasn't someone seen him? Have you got men at Headquarters to take care of calls from the public? It seems likely that some citizen might—'

'That's all taken care of, sir.'

'Mr King, would you please sign for this installation?'

King turned to Cassidy as if just discovering a Martian in his living room. '*What* installation?' he asked.

'The trunk line,' Cassidy said. 'To the main office.'

'What trunk line?'

'I told you about it before we had it installed, Mr King,' Carella said.

'Oh. Oh, yes. That.'

'I have to get a few things from you first, Mr King,' Cassidy said.

'What is it?'

'Is that the only phone in the house there? I mean, the one you had before I put in the trunk line?'

'No. We've got two numbers. That one, and my private line upstairs.'

'Could I have those numbers, please?'

'Smoke Rise 8–7214 and 7215,' King said.

'And that's it, right?'

'I've got a phone in the car, too,' King said. 'Do you want that number?'

'No, just the ones in the house. Car phone's a separate thing. We just need a record of the lines going in, so we don't get all fouled up with . . . Well, it don't make no difference. Would you sign this slip, please?' He handed it to King.

'This seems like a waste of time to me,' King said, writing. 'Once they turn the boy loose . . .'

'We're taking every precaution, Mr King,' Carella said.

'Is that why there's a policeman outside my son's bedroom?'

'That's right. We have no idea what the kidnappers will do next, you see.'

'It doesn't seem to me they have much choice.' King handed the signed slip back to Cassidy.

'Thank you,' Cassidy said. 'Don't worry about this, Mr Reynolds. You'll have him back in a couple of hours. So long, now.' He went to the door and waved, opened it, stepped into the cold, and closed it quickly behind him.

'Reynolds, you'd better eat something now,' King said. 'Inge's ready for you in the kitchen.'

'I'm not very hungry, Mr King.'

'Dammit, man, you've got to eat! Now go ahead. Jeffry will be back before you know it.'

'All right, sir, thank you.' Reynolds started out of the room.

'Would you send Detective Parker in, Mr Reynolds?' Carella said. 'He should be in the kitchen.'

'Yes, I will,' Reynolds said.

Diane King waited until he was gone. Then she said, 'Mr Carella, the kidnappers *have* heard by now, haven't they?'

'They should have, Mrs King. It's been on all the radio and TV stations, and the afternoon papers have all put out extras on it.'

'Then it's just a waste of time, isn't it?'

'Well . . .'

'Isn't it?'

'I don't like to second-guess kidnappers,' Carella said. 'That's like second-guessing murderers.'

'But . . . you don't think they'll harm him, do you?'

'Of course they won't!' King put in. 'As far as they're concerned, this is a business deal that went sour, that's all.'

'They *might* harm him, Mrs King,' Carella said calmly. 'The same way a mugger will beat up a man when he finds out that the man isn't carrying any money.'

'But that would be senseless,' King said. 'I'm sure they'll simply turn him loose the moment they hear the news.'

'Well, that's a possibility, of course,' Carella said.

'But the other is a possibility too, isn't it?' Diane said. 'That they might first hurt him? Before they release him?'

'It's a possibility,' Carella said.

'A stupid possibility. I can't believe these men are stupid.'

'Kidnappers don't have to be smart, Mr King. Only ruthless.'

'We hadn't thought of that, Doug. That they might hurt him before they turn him loose,' Cameron said. 'It's a definite possibility.'

'Yes,' Carella said. 'And there's also a *third* possibility.'

'My name is Jeffry Reynolds,' the boy said.

Sy grabbed the front of his sweater and said, 'You're lying.'

'I'm not lying. My name is Jeff Reynolds. Hey, let go that sweater, will you? It doesn't belong to me. I'm supposed to—'

'You're a lying little bastard!' Sy said, and he shoved out at Jeff, sending him sprawling across the room.

'Sy!' Kathy screamed, and she took a step toward the boy.

'Get away from him,' Sy said, moving between them.

'I'm . . . I'm not lying,' Jeff said. 'Why should I lie?' He was beginning to get a little frightened now. He kept staring at Sy, not wanting to be shoved again, yet not knowing how to prevent it. Telling the truth seemed to be the wrong course of action. And yet he did not know which lie the man wanted.

'What's your father's name?' Sy asked.

'Ch-Charles.'

'What's your mother's name?'

'My mother is dead.'

'Where do you live?'

'On Mr King's estate.'

'Don't call him Mr King!' Sy shouted. 'You know he's your father.'

'My father? No. No, he's *Bobby's* father.'

Sy seized the front of the sweater again. 'You little son of a bitch,' he said, 'don't get smart with me.'

'But I'm telling you the—'

'Shut up! I know you're Bobby King, and I don't have to— What's that?'

'What?' Jeff said, truly frightened now. 'What? What?'

'In the sweater. There. Take off that sweater.' He pulled it over Jeff's head roughly, and then turned it in his hands. A slow smile crossed his face. 'So you're Jeff Whatever-the-hell, huh?'

'Yes.'

'Sure. And the name tape in your sweater says Robert King! You lying little . . .'

'That's Bobby's sweater!' Jeff said. 'Mrs King lent it to me.'

'Tell the truth!'

'I *am* telling the truth.'

'What does your father do?'

'He's a chauffeur.'

'What were you doing in the woods?'

'I was playing with Bobby.'

'And your name is Jeff, huh?'

'Yes. Yes.'

'Why didn't you mention all this before? How come you waited for the police call?'

'I didn't know. I thought – You said you had a gun for me.'

Sy nodded. He stood with his hands on his hips, a small dapper man badly in need of a shave, watching Jeff calmly, nodding, nodding. And then, suddenly, viciously, his hand lashed out, the palm catching Jeff across the cheek.

'You're full of crap!' he yelled.

'Eddie, stop him!' Kathy shouted.

Sy advanced on the boy. 'No snotnose is gonna try pulling the wool over my eyes!'

Jeff rushed into Kathy's arms, and at last the tears came, tears of fear and frustration. 'I *am* Jeff Reynolds,' he sobbed. 'I am, I am . . .'

'Shut up!' Sy said. 'Another word out of you, and you won't be *nobody*!'

'Lay off, Sy,' Eddie said. 'The kid's scared.'

'What the hell do I care if he's scared? You think he's gonna make a fool outta—'

'I said lay off.' Sy glared at him but stopped his advance. 'Let me see the sweater, Sy.' Sy tossed the sweater to Eddie. Eddie looked at the name tape. 'It *does* say Robert King, Kathy.'

'And the boy says he borrowed it. Is that so hard to accept?'

'Yeah,' Sy said. 'With five hundred grand at stake, yeah, it's goddamn hard to accept.'

'Let's take the boy back,' Kathy said softly.

'Now hold it a minute. Let's just hold it one goddamn minute. We're not—'

'He's the wrong boy, Eddie,' Kathy said plaintively. 'Why stick your neck out? What can you gain?'

'Now, look,' Sy said, 'we're in this together, right, Eddie boy? Fifty-fifty, right? So let's calm down, okay. We can't turn this kid loose.' He paused, looking first at Kathy and then to her husband. 'He *knows* us, for Pete's sake. He can lead the bulls right to us!'

'Who said we were turning him loose?' Eddie asked.

'Nobody said so,' Sy said quickly, 'but don't even let the idea get in your head. This is a sweet setup. Let's not ruin it because a dame gets hysterical.'

'I'm just trying to figure, that's all,' Eddie said.

'Okay, nothing wrong with that,' Sy said. 'But figure *right*! Our plan calls for two guys.'

'I know. I know.'

'Okay. And we've got five hundred grand invested in this kid, remember that!'

'You've got nothing invested but a little time,' Kathy said. 'What have his parents got invested in him? What have—'

'Time is right, baby. You know how *much* time we'd do on a kidnapping rap? Provided we don't get the chair? This ain't busting into a goddamn cash register!'

'Yeah,' Eddie said. 'Kathy, he's right. We *got* to hold the kid. At least until . . .'

'We don't have to! We could turn him loose right this minute!'

'Sure, and go straight to jail!' Sy said. He turned to Eddie. Seductively, he said, 'Your share of this is two hundred and fifty thousand bucks, Eddie. You know how much money that is?'

'Who wants it?' Kathy shouted. 'We don't need it!'

'Sure, she don't need it. Lady Rockefeller. Wearing a sweater with torn elbows. She don't need it!'

'I don't!'

'Well, I do,' Eddie said softly. 'That's all the money in the world. Why shouldn't I have it?' His voice rose. 'Am I supposed to be a two-bit punk for the rest of my life? What's wrong with making a grab for that kind of loot? I want it! I want that money.'

'Then don't get talked out of it,' Sy said quickly.

'What the hell, was I born with a Smoke Rise estate like this kid? What did I get, Kathy? South Nineteenth Street and David Avenue. An old man who played the numbers, and an old lady who was a rummy!'

'You can't blame this boy for—'

'I'm not blaming nobody. I'm saying I *had* nothing, and I *still* got nothing – even after all the lousy cheap stickups. Don't I ever get nothing? Ever? When the hell do I get my chance?'

'This *is* your chance, Eddie. Turn the boy loose. Then we'll . . .'

'Then we'll what? Get to Mexico? On what? Hope? Love? And do what when we get there? The same thing I'm doing here?'

'A quarter of a million bucks, boy,' Sy said. 'It'll buy

all the radio equipment you need, all the schooling. Man, you can own a whole damn radio *station*!'

'No, just . . . just a place on the beach, maybe – for me and Kathy – where . . . where I can set up . . . you know . . . with the ocean, and maybe a little boat, I don't know.' Eddie turned to Kathy, and she saw something in his eyes she had never seen there before, a look bordering on tears. 'But *mine*, Kathy. *Mine*. A place I could *own*.'

'And a Caddy, man,' Sy said, 'with them fins sticking up in the air like sharks! And fancy clothes, and a mink for the bride, how's that? Blond mink! And a string of pearls a mile long!'

'If only . . .'

'Anything, Eddie! Anything you want, boy! The world on a string! A quarter of a million bucks!'

'We got to go ahead with this, Kathy. We got to!'

'Now you're talking,' Sy said.

'But . . . but he's the *wrong boy*!' Kathy said.

'No. No,' Eddie answered. 'He . . . he ain't the wrong boy.'

'Eddie, you *know* he is. Why . . .'

'When you stop to figure it,' Sy said softly, 'what difference does it make?'

The room went suddenly still.

'What?' Eddie said.

'Whether we got the wrong kid or not.'

'I don't follow.'

'Simple. We tried for the King kid, didn't we? Okay, E for effort. Maybe we goofed. What difference does it make? We want five hundred grand. Does a lousy chauffeur have that kind of dough?'

'No, of course he—'

'All right, who's *got* the dough?' Sy waited for an answer and then gave it himself. 'King, that's who. Okay. We call King again. We tell him we don't care whether this is his kid or his chauffeur's kid or even his goddamn gardener's kid. We want the money!'

'We'll ask *King* for it?'

'Who we gonna ask? The chauffeur?'

Eddie shook his head. 'He won't pay, Sy.'

'He'll pay, all right.'

'No.' Eddie kept shaking his head. 'He won't. Maybe Kathy's right. Maybe we ought to . . .'

'Because if he don't pay,' Sy said, 'this little boy here is going to be in a goddamn big heap of trouble.' He paused and grinned at Jeff. 'And I don't think Mr King would want blood on his hands.'

7.

WHEN LIEUTENANT PETER Byrnes left the squadroom of the 87th Precinct, the telephones were jangling as if the place were an illegal racing room taking bets before the Kentucky Derby. He walked down the corridor to the end of the hall and then down the steps leading to the muster room. He nodded at Sergeant Dave Murchison, who sat behind the high desk, and then went out into the street, where a squad car and a driver were waiting for him. It was damn cold outside. Byrnes wrapped his muffler about his throat and pulled his fedora down more tightly on his head, as if this would serve as a buffer against the cold blasts which drove across Grover Park to lash the grimy stone front of the precinct building.

The patrolman got out of the car, ran to the sidewalk and opened the door for Byrnes. Byrnes nodded, slid on to the seat and thrust his hands into his coat pockets. He was a man built with all the compactness of a travelling iron, hard as steel, capable of giving off tremendous heat in the press of any situation, adaptable to the myriad currents that moved in the precinct under his command.

'Where to, sir?' the patrolman asked, getting in behind the wheel.

'Smoke Rise,' Byrnes said. 'The kidnapping.'

The kidnapping. Even the word rankled Byrnes. He

had a grown son of his own, and he knew the torments and thrills of raising a child, and he did not hold with that part of the penal law which specified 'Provided, however, that the jury upon returning a verdict of guilty against a person upon whom the death penalty would otherwise be imposed, may recommend imprisonment of the convicted person, in lieu of death.' Nor did he hold with the further wording of Section 1250, to wit: 'Provided, further, that notwithstanding the foregoing provisions of this section with respect to punishment by death, if the kidnapped person be released and returned alive prior to the opening of the trial, the death penalty shall not apply nor be imposed . . .'

Dammit, either there *was* a death penalty or there *wasn't*. A kidnapper was the lowest form of animal life, even lower than a narcotics peddler – and Byrnes had particular reason to despise any and all pushers. And if anything was going to stop the crime of stealing another man's child, the death penalty was that deterrent. Kidnapping, by its very nature, was usually a premeditated crime. Careful planning went into the actual snatch, careful psychological manipulation went into the demands made of the parents, the slow torture of uncertainty. Byrnes would rather have seen all murderers get off with prison sentences. For whereas the thin line of premeditation separated many second-degree homicides from first-degree homicides, there was very rarely a kidnapping case in which the entire filthy crime was not thoroughly and fastidiously premeditated.

'Anywhere along here, sir?' the patrolman asked.

'What's that up ahead?' Byrnes asked.

'Looks like a light, sir.'

'Pull up over there.'

'Yes, sir.'

The patrolman eased the car to a stop. Byrnes got out and walked to where Hawes and Kronig were squatted close to the ground.

'Cotton,' Byrnes said. 'Kronig. How are you?'

'Fine, Lieutenant,' Hawes said.

'Making a cast,' Kronig said. 'Looks like it's gonna be a good one.'

'Good. Those bastards call again?'

'Not that I know of, Pete,' Hawes said. 'I've been outside quite a while.'

'Where are the rest of the men?'

'Carella and Parker are up at the house. I think Meyer broke for dinner.'

'Okay,' Byrnes said. 'I put in a call to the Chief of Detectives, and he may be out.'

'May?' Kronig said, surprised.

'He's up to his ears in this income tax thing that broke yesterday. He's been waiting for a long time to clap that hoodlum behind bars.'

'Still, a kidnapping . . .' Kronig began.

'The trouble with most crimes,' Byrnes said, 'is that they don't respect any other crimes. Nothing gets priority. In any case, if the Chief shows up, I'll be—' and he stopped talking.

A figure was coming up the road. In the darkness, the men saw only a hulking shape against the sky. Byrnes's hand slipped inside the flap of his coat. Nearly all of the detectives on the 87th – with the exception of a few who were left-handed and a few who were stubborn – wore their holsters clipped to the left side of their belts during the winter months. This eliminated the necessity of delay in unbuttoning a coat, and whereas a cross-body draw was slower than a straight one, there were very rarely any wild-West theatrics which necessitated a split-second edge. On the other hand, a cop could be dead in the time it took him to unbutton his coat far enough to reach his gun. The figure came closer as Byrnes's hand tightened on the butt of the .38.

'That you, Loot?' a voice called into the darkness.

Byrnes recognized the voice as Parker's. His hand relaxed. 'Yeah, what is it?'

'Nothing. Carella was just asking a while ago whether you got here or not. How's the squad? I'll bet things are jumping.'

'They're jumping, all right.' Byrnes turned his attention back to Kronig, and then his eyes scanned the ground, coming to rest on two large boulders near the edge of the cut-off. He walked to the rocks, knelt by them and then said, 'Can you bring that light here a minute, Cotton?'

'What is it, Lieutenant?'

'Unless I'm mistaken . . .'

The light swung over to illuminate the boulders.

In the living room, the telephone rang.

'I'll get it,' King said, moving toward the phone.

'Wait a minute!' Carella shouted. He picked up the headphones attached to the wiretap equipment and then turned to Cameron. 'Mr Cameron, get on the trunk line. If this is the kidnapper, tell them to start tracing immediately. Okay, Mr King, answer it.'

King picked up the phone. 'Hello?'

'King?'

Carella nodded at Cameron. Instantly, Cameron picked up the receiver of the trunk line telephone.

'This is Mr King,' King said.

Into his phone, Cameron said, 'Hello? We've got him on the phone now. Get started.'

'All right, King, listen. We don't care whose kid this is, you got that? We heard the radio, and we don't care. He's still alive and well, and we still want that money. You get it by tomorrow morning or the kid won't see the sun go down.'

'You want . . . ?' King started, and there was a sharp click on the line.

Carella ripped off the earphones. 'Forget it, he's gone. Dammit, I was afraid this would happen.' He went to the phone and began dialling.

'What happened?' Cameron asked, hanging up his phone.

Diane, puzzled, looked at her husband. 'Is . . . is Jeff all right?'

'Yes. Yes, he's fine,' King said.

'Hello, Dave,' Carella said, 'this is Steve. Can you get me the lieutenant right away?'

'You're sure he's all right?' Diane asked, staring at King.

'Yes, dammit, he's fine!'

'I'll tell Reynolds,' she said, and she started for the kitchen.

'Diane!'

'Yes?'

'They . . . they want me to pay the ransom. They know they've got Jeff, but they still want me to pay. They want *me* to . . .'

'We'll do whatever they say,' Diane said. 'Thank God

Jeff's all right.' And she left the room. King stared after her, a frown on his forehead.

'What?' Carella said into the phone. 'Well, how long ago did he leave, Dave? I see. Then he should be here by now. I'll check outside. How's it going back there? Murder, huh? Okay, thanks, Dave.' He hung up. 'I'm going outside, see if I can scare up the lieutenant. If that phone rings, don't answer it,' Carella said. He took his coat from the hall closet. 'Detective Meyer should be back soon. Do whatever he says.'

'About this new demand,' King said. 'I think—'

'I want to talk to the lieutenant first,' Carella said, and he rushed out of the house.

'That guy knew we'd try to trace the call,' Cameron said. 'That's why he got off the line so fast.'

'Yes,' King said. The frown on his face had given way to a slightly dazed expression now. 'Yes.'

'That means we're dealing with professionals. But why would pros pull a thing like this, asking *you* to pay?'

'I . . . I don't know.'

'Hell, if you pay them – why, your Boston deal'll go right out the window, won't it?'

'Yes. Yes, it will.'

The doorbell chimed. King started for the door, but it opened before he reached it.

'Hi, Mr King,' Meyer said. 'Boy, it's turned cold out there.' He took off his hat and coat and hung them in the closet.

'Detective Carella went outside to find the lieutenant,' King said. 'He said—'

'I know. I ran into him on the way in. What was all the excitement about?'

'The kidnappers just called again,' King said.

'Yeah?'

'They want me to pay the ransom.'

'What do you mean? Do they know they got the wrong kid?'

'Yes.'

'And they still . . . ?'

'Yes.'

'First time I ever heard of a dodge like that,' Meyer said, shaking his head. 'This just about beats it all. This means that any crook can go out and steal any kid in the world, and then send a ransom demand to the richest guy he can think of.' He shook his head again. 'Screwy, all right. But nobody says kidnappers have to be normal, huh?' He shook his head again. '*Meshugah*. Plain *meshugah*.'

'What are our chances of getting him back, Detective Meyer?'

'That's hard to say, Mr King. We don't get kidnappings every day of the week, you know. What I mean is, it's a little hard to come up with actual statistics. I can tell you that the Department is working like crazy on it. Even the Sands Spit cops and the cops in the adjoining states are going on a round-the-clock schedule.'

'What about the F.B.I.?' Cameron asked.

'They don't come in till a week's gone by,' Meyer said. 'I think Carella explained that to you, Mr King.'

'Yes.'

'But we've got them on standby.'

'Would you say the boy's chances are good?'

'I don't know,' Meyer said. 'He may be dead already, for all we know.'

'We can't assume that,' Cameron said quickly. 'There'd be no sense paying the ransom if we assumed the boy was dead.'

'Mr Cameron, they may have killed him five minutes after they picked him up,' Meyer said. 'It's been done before. Figure it out for yourself. The safest kidnap victim, from the standpoint of the criminals, is a dead one. We may deliver the ransom and then find the boy in a ditch someplace.'

'In your opinion,' King said slowly, 'would paying the ransom help the boy at all?'

'If he's alive, it certainly would. If he's dead, nothing's going to help him. But the ransom bills might help in eventually catching the kidnapper.'

'I see.'

Diane came in from the kitchen. 'Doug . . .' she started, and the doorbell chimed. 'I'll get it,' she said, changing her course.

Urgently, Cameron said, 'Doug, the boy's still alive. And your money will keep him that way, remember that!'

Diane closed the door and then came into the living room. 'A telegram, Doug,' she said. 'Addressed to us.'

'You'd better let me take that,' Meyer said, 'before anyone else handles it.' He spread a handkerchief over his hand and took the telegram. 'Got a letter opener, Mr King?'

'Yes. On the dropleaf desk there.'

Meyer went to the desk. Pinning the telegram with his handkerchief, he slit the envelope, extricated the handkerchief, draped it over his hand again and, with all the dexterity of a puppeteer, reached into the envelope for the message. Still using the handkerchief, he unfolded it, read it, and then put the handkerchief back into his pocket. 'It's okay, Mr King. You can have it.'

He handed the message to King. Diane walked over to him, and together they read the wire:

PLEASE ACCEPT DEEPEST SYMPATHY YOUR MISFORTUNE. WE WILL ADD $1000 CASH TO RANSOM IF KIDNAPPERS WILL AGREE TO RETURN BOY AT ONCE. WIRE US 27–145 HALSEY AVENUE, CALM'S POINT.
MR AND MRS THEODORE SCHAEFFER

'What is it, Doug?' Cameron asked, and King handed him the wire.

'Mr and Mrs Theodore Schaeffer,' King said. 'Nobody I know.' He paused. 'But why send it to us? Our son wasn't kidnapped.'

'Half the people out there probably *still* think it was Bobby,' Cameron said, putting the wire down on the desk.

'Let me have that,' Diane said. 'I think Reynolds would like to see it. He . . . he expected them to turn Jeff loose and now . . . he's . . . he's just sitting at the kitchen table in a kind of shock. Let me show it to him. It's such a wonderful, human offer.'

King picked up the wire and handed it to his wife.

'And then I'll send a return wire,' Diane said, 'thanking them for their concern.' She started out of the room, the telegram in her hand. She stopped and turned to face King. 'Doug, have you called the bank yet?' she asked.

'No, not yet.'

'Don't you think . . . ?'

'Mommy?'

Diane turned toward the steps. Bobby King, wearing pyjamas and robe, stood on the landing.

'What is it, darling?'

'Why is there a policeman outside my room?' Bobby asked.

'Just to make sure that everything is all right,' Diane said.

'Because of what happened to Jeff?'

'Yes, Bobby.'

'Daddy, are you getting Jeff back?'

'What? I'm sorry, son, I didn't hear . . .'

'He's my best friend. You are getting him back, aren't you?'

'Your daddy's taking care of everything,' Diane said. 'Now come, I'll put you back to bed.'

'I want Daddy to tuck me in,' Bobby said.

'Doug? Will you?'

'Sure,' Preoccupied, King walked to the steps and took his son's hand. 'Come on, Bobby.'

'Poor Bobby,' Diane said, when they were out of sight. 'He still isn't quite sure about what happened. He only knows that his friend is gone, and I think he feels responsible somehow. The way I do.'

'You've no reason to feel guilty, Diane,' Cameron said. 'Once Doug pays the ransom . . .'

'Yes, I know, but I *do* feel guilty. I almost feel as if my own son is out there with those men.' She paused. 'I'd better show Reynolds this wire.' She paused again. 'Detective Meyer, I wonder if you'd come talk to him, fill him in a little on what's being done. He's so terribly shaken by all this.'

'Sure,' Meyer said. 'Be happy to.' As they walked out

of the room, he called over his shoulder, 'If that phone rings, yell for me. Don't answer it.'

'Okay,' Cameron said.

Alone in the living room, Cameron lighted a cigarette and then walked quickly to the steps, looking upstairs. He crossed the room rapidly then, looking over his shoulder toward the kitchen, walking directly to the telephone. He dialled with quick flicks of his forefinger, his eyes never leaving the steps leading to the upstairs wing of the house. Impatiently, he tapped on the telephone table.

'Hello?' he said at last. 'May I speak to Mr Benjamin, please.' He paused. 'This is Peter Cameron. Yes, I'll wait, but please hurry.' He glanced nervously toward the steps. The hand with the cigarette stopped its tapping, moved to his mouth. He sucked in on the cigarette, blew out a steady stream of smoke, looked toward the kitchen again, and was ready to hang up when the voice came onto the line.

'Hello?'

'George?'

'This is George Benjamin.'

'Pete Cameron. I've got to make this fast. Do I still get Doug's job?'

'I offered it, didn't I? I'll put it in writing, if you like.'

'I'd like. The Boston thing I called you about earlier – it is a stock deal. Doug's cornering nineteen per cent of the voting stock.'

'What!'

'And he already owns twenty-eight per cent himself. You underestimated him, George.'

'Twenty-eight . . .' There was a long silence on the

line. 'Then how can we vote him out? How the hell can we?'

'You can't,' Cameron said. 'Unless you tell the Old Man that Doug is finagling a deal behind his back. Get the Old Man on your side temporarily. It's the only way.'

'What good will that do? If Doug's stock deal goes through, he'll be sitting with forty-seven per cent of the stuff! Even *with* the Old Man's stock, we couldn't outvote him. Hell, he could get rid of *us*.'

'*If* the deal goes through. Have you been listening to the radio?'

'This kidnapping nonsense?' Benjamin said. 'What's that got to do with—'

'It has a lot to do with it.'

'It isn't even Doug's son!'

'No, but they've asked him for the ransom, anyway. If he pays, his Boston deal goes out the window.'

'Will he pay?'

'No question about it. But in the meantime, I'm trying to find out whom he's dealing with in Boston. Maybe we can beat him to the punch.'

'You're all right, Pete,' Benjamin said admiringly.

'I know I am,' Cameron answered. 'Do what I advised, George. Get to the Old Man and clasp hands with him. If Doug's deal folds and you still want him out, you're going to need a bigger club than you've got now.'

'I'll do that. And I won't forget this.'

'I'm banking on that. I've got to hang up now, George.'

'All right.'

There was a click on the line. Smiling, Cameron

replaced the receiver and lighted a fresh cigarette. He was still smiling when the doorbell chimed. He looked up at the steps, shrugged, and went to the door, opening it. A small man wearing a black overcoat and derby stood there. A black umbrella was slung over the man's arm. There was an air of secrecy about the man, the look of a Scotland Yard operative who had worked on the Jack the Ripper case. The man was easily sixty years old, perhaps older.

'Yes?' Cameron said.

'Mr King?'

'No. I'm Mr King's assistant.'

'I would like to see Mr King, please. On business.'

'What sort of business?'

'Personal business. You may tell him that Score is here. Adrian Score.'

'Just a moment, Mr Score. I'll see if he's free. Have a seat, won't you?'

'Thank you,' Score said. He walked into the living room, holding his umbrella clutched in both hands like a timid batter facing a no-hit pitcher. He studied one of the chairs as if he suspected some wild animal had befouled it, and then sat daintily on its edge. Cameron went to the steps and called, 'Doug!'

'What is it?'

'A Mr Score to see you. On business.'

'I don't know any Mr Score,' King answered.

'Tell him it's personal,' Score said over his shoulder.

'Says it's personal, Doug.'

'Okay, I'll be right down,' King said.

'Make yourself comfortable, Mr Score,' Cameron said, walking into the living room.

'Thank you, I will. This is a lovely home.'

'Thank you.'

'Thank you,' Score repeated.

King came down the steps. 'Now what is it, Pete?' Cameron shrugged. In a whisper, he said, 'Says it's personal. I'd better go get a cup of coffee.' He started toward the kitchen.

'That phone hasn't rung again, has it?'

'No. Bobby asleep?'

'Yes.'

'I'll be in the kitchen,' Cameron said, and he went out.

'Mr Score?'

'Mr King?'

'Yes.' King extended his hand.

Score rose, shook hands briefly, and nodded curtly. 'Adrian Score, sir,' he said. 'The man who always knows the score, eh?'

'Sit down, Mr Score,' King said. Score sat. 'Now then, what's on your mind?'

'Business, Mr King.'

'It's a little late for a business call, isn't it?'

'It's never too late for business, is it, Mr King?'

'Well, that depends. What sort of business did you have in mind, Mr Score?'

'Kidnapping, Mr King.'

The room went dead silent.

'What . . . what about kidnapping?'

'Do you want your son back, Mr King?'

'My son wasn't kidnapped,' King said.

'Ah-ah, Mr King,' Score said, wagging the umbrella, 'let's be honest with each other, eh? We are both businessmen, are we not? Very well then. You can tell the newspapers what you wish, but you are now dealing with Adrian Score. Honesty, eh? I asked you a question.'

'And I gave you an answer.'

'That's what I like, Mr King. Hardheaded business. Who is this Adrian Score, you are undoubtedly asking yourself. Who is this man who comes into my house in the middle of the night and asks me if I want my son back? And you've every right to ask that, Mr King, every right in the world. Sound business tactics.' He paused, nodded, put the umbrella between his legs and said, 'Well, I will tell you who Adrian Score is. Adrian Score is the man who's going to get your son back.'

'You know where the Reynolds boy is?' King asked.

Score chuckled and put a finger alongside his nose. 'All right, sir, never argue with a client, that's Score's motto. If you prefer, he's your chauffeur's son, and a very clever ruse indeed, if I may be permitted to say so. But we both know the truth, don't we, eh? In any case, you *do* want the boy back?'

'What do you know about this?'

'Ah-ah, Mr King, I asked you a question. Do you want the boy back?'

'Of course we do!'

'Now, now, don't get excited, Mr King. Don't raise your voice. If you want the boy back, Adrian Score is your man.' He paused. 'I know who kidnapped the boy, Mr King.'

Again, the room went silent.

'Who?' King asked.

'That's the big question, eh? Who? Well, Score's got the answers, and Score can get the boy back, now what do you think of that, sir? Back home safe and sound, eh? Now how would you like that?'

'I'd like that fine. Who . . . ?'

'My services are available for the asking, Mr King. Simply ask, and Score will oblige. Score will put his talents to the task of getting your boy back for you . . .'

'Well, who . . . ?'

'. . . at a nominal fee.'

'I see.'

'Yes, Mr King. I imagined you would.'

'How much?'

'Can we measure the safety and well-being of a toddler in terms of cold cash, Mr King?'

'The boy's father is a chauffeur. The five-hundred-thousand-dollar demand is far beyond his—'

'Mr King, please, please,' Score said, as if he could not tolerate the lie a moment longer. 'Please.' He leaned forward, his hands clasped over the handle of the umbrella. His voice dropped to a whisper. Intently, he said, 'I am ready to establish contact with the kidnappers, *whose* identity is already known to me, sir, and I will ascertain that the boy is alive and well, serving as a liaison between the principals, negotiating for the ransom payment, seeing that every term of the contract is strictly adhered—'

'Goddammit, how much?'

'Five thousand dollars, Mr King.'

'In addition to the exorbitant ransom demand?'

'I was thinking I might – But no, that would be far too risky.'

'What?' King asked eagerly.

'Perhaps, were you to deliver the five thousand dollars to me at once, I could get the boy back now. Tonight. Without necessity for further payment.'

'How would you manage that?'

'We are both businessmen, Mr King,' Score said, smiling. 'But does Macy's tell Gimbels?'

'Who has the boy?'

'Business, business, Mr King. Cash on the barrelhead in Score's Store.'

'How do I know you can get him back?'

'You shall have to accept my word for that, Mr King.'

'In business, Mr Score, I accept *no one's* word.'

'An admirable trait, to be sure. But a good businessman knows when his back is to the wall, Mr King. And surely you can see I'm a man to trust. You realize the danger of my position, do you not, sir?'

King's attention was momentarily diverted by Meyer Meyer, who had entered behind Score and stopped in the archway leading from dining room to living room. Score, apparently, had not seen the change of expression on King's face. Blithely unaware of Meyer's presence, he continued with his monologue

'Surely you appreciate the danger of my position, surely you do. If these ruthless men were to suspect that I was planning to get the boy away from them, my life would be placed in instant jeopardy. These men are hardened criminals, sir, cut-throats who would stop at nothing short of—

'*Which* men, Score?' Meyer called from the archway.

'Eh?' Score said, and he whirled in his seat to face the archway.

'Which men were you talking about, Score?' Meyer said.

Score studied Meyer painstakingly. 'I do not believe I've had the pleasure, sir,' he said.

'How'd you sneak past our men at the gate, Score?'

'Perhaps, Mr King, you would do me the honour of introducing this gentleman. He seems to have made an error in—'

'I'll introduce myself, Score, even though we've already met. Detective Second Grade Meyer Meyer of the Eighty-seventh Squad. Ring a bell?'

'Charmed, I'm sure,' Score said.

'I see you're still disguised as a leech.'

'Eh?'

'This is one of the biggest con men in the business, Mr King, and he specializes in human grief. If someone's kid is missing for as long as an hour, you can bet Adrian Score will be on the scene with some scheme for getting the kid back. At a nominal fee, of course.'

'This is absurd, Mr King. Surely two businessmen should be able to discuss—'

'Get the hell out of here, you rotten louse! Get out before I arrest you as an accessory to a kidnapping!'

'Accessory to a . . . ?'

'Yes, accessory!' Meyer yelled. 'A person who wilfully gives false information concerning a kidnapping while knowing that information to be false!'

'False . . . false . . . information?' Score squeaked.

'Get out, Score! I'm warning you!'

'Really, Mr King. I am a guest in your home, a respected businessma—'

'*Move!*' Meyer shouted.

Score rose rapidly and handed King a small white rectangle. 'My card, sir.' Backing off toward the door, he said, 'Call me anytime, sir, anytime at all. The name is Score. Adrian Score.' He opened the front door, shot a hasty glance at Meyer and then shouted, '*I can get your boy back!*' and slammed the door behind him.

'That rotten parasite!' Meyer said.

'He called us both businessmen,' King said. 'Why, he was nothing but a crook!'

'One of the worst. Human feelings mean nothing to him. But hang around a while, Mr King. Score is only the beginning. We'll be getting a wide range of ransom demands soon. Every filthy crook who's looking for a soft touch will hop on the bandwagon as soon as he figures a gimmick. The woods'll be full of kidnappers. We won't know the real bastards from the fake ones.'

'How do we know we have the real one now?' King asked.

'We don't. We can only assume we do.' Meyer paused and shook his head. 'One thing's for sure.'

'What's that?'

'I sure as hell wouldn't like to be back at the squad answering telephones right now.'

'Eighty-seventh Squad, Detective Willis?'

''Allo, you know the kidnap, please?'

'Who is this?' Willis said.

'Who you?' the woman said.

'Detective Willis. Can I help you, lady?'

'My name issa Miz Abruzzi,' the woman said. 'I'ma see the li'la boy.'

'The kidnap victim?'

'Yas, yas. He wass inna diner with two men. Both needa shaves, you unnerstan'? He's a li'la blond boy, no?'

'Yes, that's right.' Willis paused. 'When did you see him, lady?'

'When you tink?'

'Well, I don't know. You tell me.'

'This morn'.'

'Yeah, well the boy wasn't missing until this afternoon.'

'I see,' Mrs Abruzzi said, and then, unperturbed, she said, 'I wassa sit in the boot', an' these two men they come in wit' the boy. So right away, I'ma tink this is the li'la boy he wassa kidnap. So I watch what they—'

'Yes, Mrs Abruzzi, thank you very much,' Willis said, and he hung up. 'Holy God,' he shouted to Arthur Brown, 'I never saw anything like this in my life. You'd think we were giving away gold dollars to anybody who called Frederick 7–8024.'

'Everybody wants to help,' Brown said. 'The trouble is—' The phone on his desk rang. He picked it up quickly. 'Eighty-seventh, Detective Brown speaking.'

'I'd like the lieutenant, Detective Brown.'

'He's not here. Who's this, please?'

'Where is he?'

'Who'm I talking to?' Brown asked.

'This is Cliff Savage. I'm a reporter. The lieutenant knows me.'

'Well, he's still not here, Mr Savage. What can I do for you?'

'On this kidnapping.'

'Yes?'

'Is it true that the kidnappers have asked King for the ransom? Even though they know they've got the wrong boy?'

'I don't know what's going on out there, Mr Savage. I'm sorry.'

'Well, look, how can I find out?'

'Call me back later.'

'Where's the lieutenant? At the King house?'

'I wouldn't call there, Mr Savage. They probably want to keep those lines free for any possible contact from the—'

'The public has a right to know what's going on!' Savage said.

'Listen, you want to argue with me?'

'No, but . . .'

'Then don't. I feel like I've been working in the telephone room of the Automobile Club on the night a truck spilled a full load of tacks all over the highway. I'm getting a cauliflower ear from this goddamn phone, Mr Savage, and you sure as hell aren't helping it any.'

'Do you have the number out at the King house?'

'No.'

'I can find it, you know.'

'You may find trouble, too, Mr Savage. I'd keep off that phone if I were you. You may find yourself impeding the progress of an investigation.'

'Thanks, Brown. I'll do you a favour someday.'

'I can hardly wait,' Brown said, and he hung up. 'The son of a bitch,' Brown said. 'Wasn't he involved that time Reardon and Foster were killed? And Bush? Didn't he almost get Steve's wife in hot water?'

'Almost ain't the word,' Willis said. 'If he ever sets foot in this squadroom, the lieutenant'll drown him in the water cooler. Where's Miscolo? I want some coffee. Miscolo? Hey, Miscolo!'

'Yo?' a voice from the clerical office shouted.

'Make some joe.'

'What the hell you think this is?' Miscolo called. 'Howard Johnson's?'

'The coffee here is better,' Willis said flatteringly.

'Yeah, yeah,' Miscolo mumbled, but they could hear

him opening the file drawer to take out the can of coffee.

The telephone on Willis's desk rang.

'Come on,' he said to the phone, 'cut it out, willya?'

The phone kept ringing.

'Stop, stop, stop ringing.'

The phone shrieked into the room.

'All right, all right, all right,' he said, lifting the receiver. 'Eighty-seventh Squad, Willis. What? You saw the boy? . . . Yes, he's a blond boy . . . Yes, he's about eight . . . Yes, he was wearing a red sweater . . . Yes, sir. Yes, that certainly does sound like him . . . Yes, sir, where did you see him, sir? . . . Where, sir? . . . In a movie, sir? Which movie, sir? . . . I see. And he was sitting in the audience, is that right? . . . He wasn't? Well, then . . .' Willis paused, and an amazed look crossed his face. 'He was *in* the picture?' he said. 'You mean he was *acting* in the picture. On the screen? Mister, you mean this kid you saw – *In* the picture? Oh, mister, please, I got enough headaches.' He hung up abruptly. 'He calls me about a movie star. Says it's a remarkable coincidence. For the love of—'

The phone rang again.

'I'm gonna get a record made,' Willis said. 'It's gonna say, "Eighty-seventh Squad, Detective Willis. You saw the kid, right? Where? When? Thank you." Save my voice for the opera.' He picked up the receiver. 'Eighty-seventh Squad, Willis . . . Yes, ma'am, this is the Detective Division . . . Yes, ma'am, we are handling the Jeff Reynolds kidnapping . . . Yes, ma'am, we . . .'

The phone on Brown's desk rang.

'Eighty-seventh Squad, Detective Brown speaking . . .'

'Eighty-seventh Squad, Di Maeo . . .'

'Eighty-seventh Squad, Detective Willis . . .'

'Eighty-seventh Squad, Hernandez . . .'

'Eighty-seventh Precinct, Sergeant Murchison . . .'

'Eighty-seventh Precinct, Captain Frick . . .'

'Headquarters, Lieutenant Vinnick . . .'

'Arson Squad, Detective Hopkins . . .'

'You saw the boy, sir?'

'The boy was with three men, ma'am?'

'You saw the boy . . .'

'When, sir?'

'What street was that, sir?'

'Where, sir?'

'Where, ma'am?'

Where?

Where?

Where?

Lieutenant Byrnes walked into the Douglas King living room and blew on his hands.

'Hello, Steve,' he said. 'How's it going?'

'All right, sir,' Carella answered. 'Mr King, this is Lieutenant Byrnes.'

'How do you do, sir?' Byrnes said, and he took King's hand.

'How does it look, Lieutenant?' King asked.

'So-so. Has the Auto Squad delivered that list yet, Steve?'

'No.'

'Dammit. I understand "they're asking" you for the money, Mr King. That's a tough break.' He sighed. 'But maybe we've got something good outside.'

'What happened, Pete?'

'We're getting a good cast of a tyre track, and . . .'

'Will that help at all?' King said.

'It usually does. Tyre patterns are pretty easy to run down. Headquarters has an up-to-date file on tyre patterns, and once we get a good casting, half the battle is won. It's been our experience that a car will usually carry the same make of tyre on all four wheels – especially a new car. And, as funny as this may sound at first, when a tyre wears out, the owner will usually replace it with a tyre of the same make. So we can generally figure the make of car from the tyre pattern. In this case, we think we've got something else to go on, too.'

'What's that?' King asked.

'There are two boulders on the ground near where we found the tyre track. The guy driving that car was probably in a big hurry. He sideswiped one of the boulders. We got ourselves a pretty decent paint scraping from the rock. Kronig's already on the way to the lab with it. With a little luck, we may be able to come up with both the year and the make of the car. With a little luck. That's why I'm anxious to get that stolen-car list.'

'I see,' King said.

'I don't suppose Mr Reynolds is around, is he? I'd like to keep him abreast of what we're doing. The worst part of any kidnapping case is that the parents never feel we're doing enough.'

'He's in the kitchen, Pete,' Carella said. 'Want me to get him for you?'

'No, I'll go out to him in a few minutes.'

The doorbell chimed. Carella went to the door and

threw it open. A uniformed policeman stood there. 'I want Detective Carella,' he said.

'That's me.'

'You called the Auto Squad a little while ago?'

'Yes.'

'They sent me up with this.' He extended a manila envelope. 'A stolen-car list.'

'Thanks,' Carella said.

'What's the latest on the kid?' the patrolman asked.

'Nothing new, so far,' Carella said.

'Yeah.' The patrolman shook his head. 'Well, there's the list.'

'Thanks.'

'Okay.'

Carella closed the door behind him.

'Let me see that, Steve,' Byrnes said. He opened the manila envelope and studied the typewritten sheet. 'Not too bad. Couple of dozen cars, all told. Let's hope the lab boys turn up something that matches something on this list.'

'And where will that put you, Lieutenant?' King asked.

'Huh?'

'Suppose you know the car they used was a stolen one? How will that help you in finding the boy?'

'It'll give us something to look for. We've got roadblocks hemming in this whole city, Mr King. It would help if we knew the shape and size and colour of the needle, don't you think?'

'If they were smart enough to use a stolen car, they were probably smart enough to get rid of it immediately.'

'Unless they have further use for it,' Byrnes said.

'In which case they probably repainted it.'

'Unless there wasn't time. A homemade paint job is a pretty conspicuous thing, Mr King. The last thing these kidnappers want is to be conspicuous.'

'I see,' King said.

'I know it sounds slim, Mr King, but we haven't got a hell of a lot to work with here, and every little bit counts. Once the money is delivered, we'll have ransom bills to look for. And when we get the boy back, perhaps he'll be able to tell us something about his abductors. Unless we reach them before that.'

'Or unless the boy is dead already,' King said flatly.

'Yes. Unless he's dead. There wouldn't be any sense continuing then, would there?'

'None at all,' King answered.

'I want to talk to you about the ransom, Mr King. We can't mark the money, and there probably won't even be time to record all the serial numbers. They particularly specified no consecutive serial numbers, didn't they?'

'Yes. But . . .'

'Only to make the recording job more difficult. But we *will* be able to record some of those numbers, and even a partial list is a good thing to have. Those men will have to spend that money someday.' He paused. 'You haven't called the bank yet, have you?'

'No, I haven't.'

'Good. If you don't mind, I'd like to talk to them when you do. To tell them just what would be most helpful to us. If the F.B.I. comes in on this, they'll need—'

'I'm afraid I won't be able to help you, Lieutenant Byrnes,' King said.

Byrnes looked at him in puzzlement. 'I don't understand,' he said. 'You don't want me to talk to your bank?'

'No, Lieutenant, that's not it. I won't be talking to the bank, either.'

'Wh—?'

'I'm not going to pay the ransom, Lieutenant.'

'You're . . .' The room went silent. Byrnes looked at Carella. 'Well, of course . . . Well, that's entirely up to you. No one can force you to.'

'What are you saying, Mr King?' Carella said, frowning. 'You – you have to pay that ransom! That boy—'

'Knock it off, Steve,' Byrnes said.

'But he has to! That kid hasn't got a chance unless he—'

'I don't *have* to do anything!' King said tightly. 'Let's get this straight, gentlemen. I'm telling it to you, and I'll tell it to the kidnappers if they call again, and I'll tell it to anyone who cares to listen. I am not paying the ransom.' He paused. 'I am *not* paying the ransom.'

8.

THERE WAS ONLY one light burning in the parlour of the Sands Spit farmhouse, a standing floor lamp that stood close to the open sofa bed, casting a circle of light on the exposed wooden flooring. Jeff Reynolds was asleep in the centre of the bed. He turned and mumbled, and the blanket fell free of his shoulder. Kathy Folsom went to the bed and covered him again. Eddie Folsom lighted a cigarette and shook out the match.

'He asleep?'

'Yes.'

In the bathroom, Sy Barnard was singing at the top of his lungs. His shirt, tie, and gun holster were draped over the back of one of the parlour chairs. The police radio, part of the complicated equipment which stood against the wall, monotonously bleated its calls.

'. . . proceed to intersection of Cambria and Newbridge. We want a block there to cover the whole intersection. You'll have 311 to assist. You got that, 307?'

'We got it.'

'Car 311, Car 311, proceed to intersection of Cambria and Newbridge to assist 307 in road block.'

'This is 311, okay. Any make on the car yet?'

'Nothing, 311.'

'Right.'

'Sy!' Eddie called. 'Hey, Sy, you hear this?'

Sy, his face half covered with lather, came out of the bathroom. He was wearing only his undershirt. His arms and shoulders were covered with thick matted hair. 'What's the matter?' he said.

'They got road blocks springing up like mushrooms. How we gonna use the car?'

'What're you getting excited about? So they got roadblocks. So who cares?'

'You don't understand, Sy. They're stopping every car on the road. We have to use that car in the morning. How're we gonna . . . ?'

'How many times do I have to tell you? I'll be driving, right? Alone, right? In a lousy old Ford that don't attract any attention. So let's say they stop me. So I'm a guy on his way to work. I've got a driver's licence, and I'll show it to them if they ask for it. So? Do they know I'm driving a stolen car? How can they know that? We changed the plates, didn't we? So nobody's got nothing on me. So why the hell are you worried about their stupid roadblocks?'

'What about after we get the money?' Eddie said. 'How we gonna leave here? They'll still be watching.'

'And we'll still have nothing to worry about, because we won't have the kid with us. It'll be a guy, his wife and their brother-in-law. There's nothing to worry about. Let me finish shaving, will you? I feel like a Grade-A bum.' He went into the bathroom. Kathy waited until the door closed behind him.

'Eddie . . . after he gets the money, what'll happen to the boy?' 'We'll leave him right here. We'll call King to let him know where the kid is.'

Kathy nodded. 'That would be taking a . . . a big chance, wouldn't it?'

I don't think so.'

'Eddie, let's get out of here. Let's get out now, before it's too late!'

'Aw, honey, please, will you cut it out?'

'Car 234, Car 234, are you still at the tunnel entrance?'

'This is 234. That's where we are, Handsome.'

'Okay, okay.'

'Listen to them,' Kathy said.

'Sy says we got nothing to worry about. We've got to trust him in this, Kathy. He knows what he's doing.' Eddie walked to the ash tray and squashed out his cigarette. 'Sy never gave me a bum steer all the time I knew him. He's all right, Kathy.'

'Yes, he's fine,' she answered sarcastically.

'Well, he is. He taught me a lot.'

'Yes, he certainly taught you a lot.'

'Well, dammit, he *did*!' Eddie paused. 'He didn't have to hook up with somebody like me. Sy is big-time.'

'Big-time!' Kathy said. 'He's a hoodlum!'

'Aw, don't say that about him. He got a few bad breaks, that's all. But he's okay. Listen, you think it was easy to plan something like this? You know how many things that poor guy has on his mind?'

'He's got only one thing on his mind, Eddie.'

'Yeah? What's that?'

'He wants to kill that boy.'

'Aw, come on, willya? Wants to kill the boy! Sy's got a cool business head. He ain't yearning to get involved in a murder rap. All he wants out of this is his share of the loot.'

'And you?'

'What about me?'

'What do you want?'

'The same thing. Two hundred and fifty thousand bucks.'

'And how far will you go to get it?'

'What the hell are you talking about?' Eddie said. He went to the dresser, picked up the cigarette pack, dug into it, and crumpled it when he realized it was empty.

'How bad do you want that money, Eddie?'

'Very bad. You got a cigarette?'

Kathy opened her purse and looked into it. 'No, I haven't,' she said. She snapped the bag shut. 'Eddie, when we were kids, we used to play a game. It was called "Suppose?" and we used to say, "Suppose somebody offered you a million dollars, what would you do for it? Would you cut off a toe for it? Would you give one of your eyes? Would you spit on the cross?" Things like that. It was funny to hear the answers. All the kids had a different price for that million dollars.'

'What are you driving at?' Eddie said. 'Sy! Hey, Sy!'

'Yeah?'

'You got any cigarettes?'

Sy poked his head around the door. 'What?'

'You got any cigarettes?'

'In my jacket. You mind if I finish shaving?' He went back into the bathroom.

Eddie crossed to the jacket and went through the pockets. 'None here!' he said disgustedly. 'Sy, you ain't got any.'

'There's a carton in the car!' Sy yelled. 'Stop bothering me.'

'Where?'

'In the glove compartment. Man, will you let me shave in peace?'

Eddie started for the front door.

'What's *your* price, Eddie?'

'I don't know what you mean, Kathy.'

'Do you give an arm – but not an eye? Do you take part in a kidnapping – but stop at murder?'

The room was silent.

'What do your kid games have to do with real life?' Eddie asked at last.

'Sy is planning to kill that boy,' Kathy said.

'You're nuts.'

'It's part of his scheme, Eddie. He can't chance leaving the boy alive to identify him.' She paused. 'And I have to know where you stand.'

Eddie sighed. 'Where I stand, huh? Can't you just leave me alone?'

'No, Eddie. I have to know.'

'All right. All right, look. You were a kid, and you played your kid games and . . . and I was a kid, too, all right? Okay, and when I was a kid, I didn't have nothing. You know, Kathy? Nothing. Nothing. I . . . I . . . you say Mexico . . . you want to go to Mexico. Well, I want to go there, too. I really want to go there and . . . and I want to have a lot of money and I want waiters to treat me nice . . . and I want to have *something*. Not always nothing, all the time. I . . . I don't want to be dirt anymore, okay?'

'Okay. But—'

'So, honey, don't ask me where I stand. Don't harp on me. I don't want to start wondering about what I'm doing or why I'm doing it. This is the only way, believe me.' He paused, and when he went on there was a peculiar distress in his voice. 'This is the only way I know.'

'But it's not,' Kathy said firmly. 'Eddie, we could leave now. Sy's in the other room. If we hurried . . . Eddie, we could get out of here, and drop the boy someplace, and be free. Do you think the cops would care? If the boy is returned safely before any money changes hands, do you really think they'll try too hard to find us? We *could* get to Mexico. And we'd be together, without having to run all the time.'

'I . . . I don't know. I need a cigarette.'

'Eddie, tell me.'

'Kathy, leave me alone!' he shouted. He paused. 'I'm getting out of here.'

'Where are you going?'

'Down to the car for those cigarettes and . . . and then I'm going to take a walk.'

'I'll go with you.'

'I don't want any company. Leave me alone!' he said, and he opened the door.

'You still haven't told me where you stand, Eddie. I have to know . . .'

The door slammed on her words. She stood despondently in the centre of the room, listening to his footsteps retreating on the gravel outside. She walked to the door and locked it, and she leaned against it and sighed heavily, and suddenly Sy began singing in the bathroom again. She walked to the window and peered around the edge of the shade, stood there thoughtfully for a moment, turned to lean against the wall, facing the bathroom, studying the closed bathroom door, and then the boy asleep on the bed. When she made her decision, it showed in her face, and it showed in the sudden stiffening of her body. She took one last look at the closed bathroom door and then moved swiftly and purposefully to the sofa bed.

Seïzing Jeff's shoulder, she whispered, 'Jeff! Wake up, Jeff!'

Jeff popped upright in the bed almost instantly. 'What is it?' he said. 'What? What?'

'Shhh,' she warned. She waited, watching the bathroom. 'Be quiet and do what I tell you to do.' She paused again. 'I'm taking you out of here.'

'You're taking me home?' Jeff asked exuberantly.

'Shhhh! For God's sake, keep your voice down.' She looked at the bathroom door and then the front door. Sy's voice was raised in song. There was no sound coming from the front yard. 'I can't take you home,' Kathy said, 'but I can take you out of here. I'll drop you off somewhere. Someone will find you. You'll get home. But you have to help me, and we have to move quickly and quietly. Do you understand?'

Whispering now, Jeff said, 'Yes. Are they . . . are they going to kill me?'

'I don't know. But we're not going to give them the chance.'

'Is Eddie your husband?'

'Yes.'

'He's not so hot,' Jeff said.

'He's my—'

'But he doesn't seem as if he would hurt me,' Jeff added hastily.

The singing in the bathroom stopped abruptly. Kathy glanced at the closed door sharply. The sound of running water seeped into the silent room.

'You're pretty,' Jeff said.

'Thank you. Where's your coat?'

'I don't have a coat. Only Bobby's sweater.'

'You'll need it. It's very cold out there. Where is it?'

'On the chair there.'

Kathy walked swiftly and silently to the chair. She took the sweater and began pulling it over his head.

'We'll go straight to the road,' she said. 'When we reach the road, we're going to start running, do you understand?'

'I'm a good runner,' Jeff said.

'All right then, come on.' Quickly she put on her coat and took his hand. Together, they tiptoed to the front door. Kathy unlocked it, turning the lock with all the caution of a safecracker. The tumblers clicked, and she hesitated. Then, slowly, cautiously, she opened the door a crack. The squeak sounded like a gunshot in the silent room. She peeked into the yard and then held out her hand to Jeff again. 'Come.'

'Wait!' he said, and he pulled away from her suddenly and darted back into the room.

'What . . . ?'

'My gun!' he said, rushing to the table where the empty shotgun rested. 'He gave it to me, didn't he?'

'Yes – hurry,' she whispered impatiently.

Jeff seized the shotgun by the barrel, swinging it around as it slid off the table, starting to run for the front door simultaneously. The stock of the gun clung to the table, hit an ash tray as Jeff pulled on the barrel. And then the ash tray moved to the edge, caught by the gun's stock, rushing, tilting, sliding over the edge of the table and dropping leadenly to the floor. The crash filled the room. Scattered pieces of glass ricocheted like fragments of a hand grenade. At the door, Kathy almost screamed. She brought her hand to her mouth and bit the knuckles. Jeff froze.

'Do you think . . . ?'

'Shhh!' Kathy said.

Silently, they waited. The door to the bathroom remained closed. Quickly, Kathy opened the front door again and peeked out.

'All right, let's go,' she said, and the bathroom door opened. She did not see the door opening. Looking into the yard, her hand extended behind her, waiting for Jeff, she did not know that Sy had entered the room, stopping in the bathroom doorway, his hands on his hips, instant recognition on his face.

'Hurry, hurry,' she said to Jeff, and she beckoned with her hand and then, when she realized he was not coming to her, turned from the door, starting to say, 'Jeff, will you please—' and then spotting Sy, and going pale all at once.

'Well, well,' Sy said. 'Where do you think you're going?'

'I was taking the boy out,' Kathy said.

'Oh, was you now?' His eyes flicked the room. 'Where's Eddie?'

'He went for a walk.'

Sy went quickly to the front door, locking it. 'Is that two-bit punk planning a doublecross?'

'No. He didn't know anything about this. He went to the car for cigarettes.'

'So you figured this was as good a time as any to blow the coop, huh? Boy, leave it to a dame. Lots of curves, and they're always ready to throw one of them at you. Take off your coat!'

Kathy hesitated.

'Take it off before I rip it off!' Sy shouted.

She took off the coat and tossed it onto the bed.

'The kid, too. He won't need that sweater. He ain't going anyplace.' Kathy went to Jeff and helped him to take off the sweater. 'Real buddy-buddy, ain't you? A real nice team, you and the kid.' Sy reached into his pocket and when his hand came into view again a closed switch knife was on the palm. He pressed a stud in the knife's handle, and the blade flashed into view. Slowly, he walked to where Kathy and the boy stood near the open bed.

'Listen to me, you little bitch,' he said. 'You try anything like this again, and you're gonna need plastic surgery, you understand? No matter what your darling Eddie says. And I'll personally rip this little bastard's heart out! Now you just remember that! You just remember!'

'I'm not afraid of you, Sy,' she said.

'No, huh?' He lifted the knife so that the blade was close to her throat now. 'You better even watch the way you talk to me from now on, honey. You better be real sweet to me, and maybe I'll forget what you just tried to pull. Real sweet to me from now on.'

With the blade at her throat, Sy moved his free hand down the length of Kathy's arm, caressing her. She pulled away from him quickly. The doorknob rattled, and Kathy moved toward it.

'Hey, open up,' Eddie called from outside.

Sy gestured at the door with his head. He pressed the blade of the knife shut and returned the knife to his pocket. Kathy unlocked the door. Eddie came into the room.

'You got your cigarettes, I see,' Sy said, smiling.

'Yeah.' Eddie dragged deeply on the butt. 'Gee, it's nice out. Cold, but real clear. Full of stars.'

'That means a good day tomorrow,' Sy said. 'Even the weather's with us. There ain't nothing going to foul up this job.' His eye caught Kathy's. 'Nothing,' he repeated.

'How come the kid's up?' Eddie asked.

'The little bastard can't sleep. He's worried about what's gonna happen to him tomorrow.'

'You think it'll go all right, Sy?'

'It can't miss,' Sy said. He turned to Kathy again. 'You hear that, Kathy? It can't miss. It's gonna work, and nothing's gonna stop it. We're all gonna be rich. I'll never ride another goddamn subway as long as I live. I'll wear silk underwear. You know there are guys who wear silk underwear? Me! I'm gonna be one of them.' He nodded vigorously. 'Tell her about it, Eddie. Tell her how we worked it out. Your wife here thinks we're playing games.'

'Look, let's just do it,' Eddie said. 'What do we have to talk about it for?'

'I want her to know because it's beautiful, that's why. What the hell's the matter with you? Are you ashamed of it? It's a goddamn good plan.'

'Yeah, I know, but . . .

'We're gonna call King in the morning, and give him instructions about the drop, and there won't be a cop in this city who can stop us, or who can even *find* us!' Sy paused. 'How does that sound to you, Kathy?'

'It sounds very smart,' Kathy said tonelessly.

'Yeah, very smart. *Damn smart!* Not even King is gonna know where the hell to drop that loot, so he couldn't tell the cops even if he wanted to. All he's gonna know is that we're waiting for it. But he won't know where.' He saw the puzzlement on Kathy's face. 'Yeah,' he said. 'Yeah. And it'll work. All because of Eddie's monster there.' He pointed to the radio equipment against the wall. 'Why do you think we knocked ourselves out on these radio store jobs? To give Eddie something to play with?'

'I thought you needed a radio for listening to police calls,' Kathy said, more puzzled now.

'A setup like this? For police calls? You know what those two tin cans are over there? Oscillators. And the big thing behind them? A transmitter. Am I right, Eddie?'

'Yeah, that's right. You see, Kathy, what we're gonna do—'

'What we're gonna do,' Sy said, 'is surprise the pants off King and the cops both. Once King gets started, there ain't gonna be a soul in the world but him who knows what to do. Not the cops, not nobody. Nobody but King and us. Once he leaves the house with that money in his hands—'

'*If* he leaves the house,' Kathy said. '*If* he pays the ransom.'

'I'll let you in on a secret, sweetheart,' Sy said. 'He better leave the house, and he better pay the ransom.' His hand darted into his pocket, and the switch knife appeared again. The stud made no sound when he pressed it. The blade snicked open with a slight whisper. Sy looked at Jeff, who stood by the bed, terror wide in his eyes now.

'He just *better* pay the ransom,' Sy said softly.

9.

THE MAN IN charge of the police laboratory was Lieutenant Sam Grossman.

The lab to the casual observer was a sterile place of long white counters and tall green cabinets. The counters were washed with fluorescent light and ultraviolet light, and the cabinets were full of laundry marks and pistols and cartridges and tyre patterns and analytical charts and pieces of glass and grass and morass and anything and everything which could be used for comparison purposes against a suspect item. There were a good many suspect items which came into the lab every hour of every day. The items ranged from the headlight glass found on a highway after a hit-and-run to a bloody hand wrapped in last Sunday's real-estate section of *The New York Times*. It was not always pleasant to deal with the packages that were dropped at the lab's doorstep like orphans on a snowy Christmas Eve. There were times when the work assumed ghoulish proportions, and many a man with a weak stomach had instantly applied for transfer to the city's Bureau of Criminal Identification, or perhaps the morgue at one of the local hospitals. It was one thing, you see, to deal with violent and sudden deaths in an active, participating way. It was another to reduce death to a scientific formula, to deal with severed limbs and errant sperm cells, hair-encrusted blunt weapons, cartridges flattened by impact with bone. The imagination soared when confronted with the grisly inarticulate by-products of murder or manslaughter. A long blond hair tangled into the sharp cutting edge of an axe shrieked more loudly than the corpse of the woman lying on a slab at the morgue. Understatement, a subtle weapon of novelists since the beginning of literature, became a daily working grindstone against which the lab technicians blunted their emotions. Sam Grossman, an emotional man by nature, an unemotional man by trade, ran the lab with the uncompromising discipline of an African missionary. The lab, Grossman knew, could very often shorten the work of the men out there in the field. The lab could bring criminals to justice. And if he could help to do this, Grossman felt his life was not being wasted. Sometimes his job was extremely difficult. Sometimes, as was the case with the casting Kronig brought back, Grossman's job was exceptionally easy. He simply went to his files and came up with the right tyre pattern in less than five minutes. The record card looked like the picture overleaf.

The name of the tyre, then, was Tirubam, and it was manufactured by the Rubber Tire Corporation of America, whose offices in this city were located at 1719 Carter Avenue in Isola. The tyre had been standard equipment in 1948 on products of the General Motors Corporation. In 1949 and 1950, the Ford Motor Company had used it on its entire line. In 1954, Chrysler Motors had equipped its automobiles with this tyre. The field seemed a rather large one from which to choose.

The size of the tyre, however, was determined from the cast to be 670×15. This was a break which

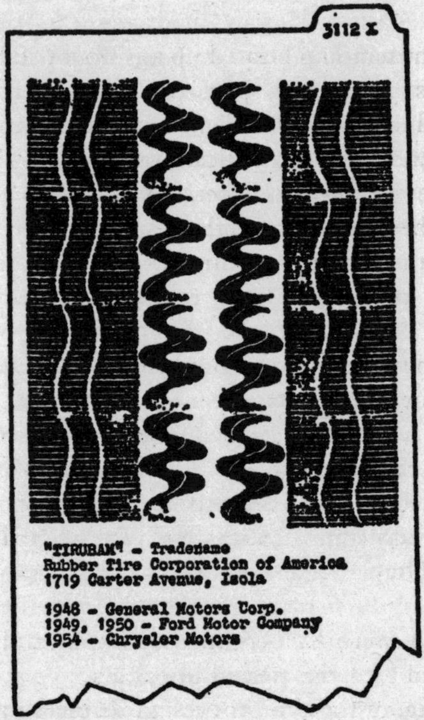

automatically eliminated any automobile manufactured before 1949, since the wheel rim had been sixteen inches in diameter up to that time and the changeover for the entire industry had come in 1949. The size of the tyre, too, eliminated any of the larger cars which both Ford and Chrysler produced in the respective years they'd used the tyres. The 1949 Mercury, for example, carried a 710×15 tyre. The 1949 Lincoln carried an 820×15. The field had been narrowed to the smallest cars produced by either of the companies in the suspect years.

The paint scraping cleared up any doubt. By the time Grossman's boys had put the sample through a spectographic examination and had made a microscopic diagnosis and a microchemical examination, they knew exactly the nature of the beast with which they were dealing. They simply took the results of their tests and compared these with facts already compiled, listed, and waiting in their files. Their record cards told them:

1. That the paint was a product of the Ford Motor Company.
2. That it was called Birch Gray by the firm.
3. That it was used on the company's 1949 models.
4. That it had been dropped in 1950 in favour of a slightly different shade which the company called Dover Grey.

Sam Grossman studied the facts. He studied them with the coldly unemotional eye of a scientist. Looking over the figures, his blue eyes guileless behind their spectacles, his face bearing the craggy, homespun look of a New England farmer, he nodded his head gently. The suspect car was a grey 1949 Ford. There was nothing more to do but call the King house and present the facts. The other policemen would take it from there. Sam Grossman took off his glasses, closed his eyes, and rubbed at them with thumb and forefinger. Then he put the glasses on again and dialled the King estate.

Meyer Meyer took the call in the living room. Douglas King, sitting in an easy chair near the fireplace, sat staring at the shifting flames while Meyer copied down the information the lab gave him. King showed no indication of listening to the call. The fire lighted the rugged planes of his face, glistened redly in the greying hair over his temples.

'I got it, Sam,' Meyer said. 'That's nice work. What? . . . Well, it doesn't look so hot on this end, but now we've got something to look for . . . . Yes, we'll get it out right away. Thanks a lot, Sam.' He hung up and turned to King. 'A grey 1949 Ford. That's what they were driving. I'd better find the lieutenant. He'll want to check this against his list.' He studied King silently for a moment. Then he said, 'Penny for your thoughts, Mr King.'

'I'm not thinking anything worthwhile at the moment, Detective Meyer,' King said.

'Mmmm. Well, I'm going outside, see if I can rustle up the lieutenant. Yell if that phone rings.'

'I will,' King promised. Meyer put on his coat and left the room. King did not look up when the door eased shut. He kept staring into the flames as if his soul were there, as if he could read himself in the leaping reds and yellows. When Diane King came into the room, he still did not look up. She walked directly to him and stood before him, blocking his view of the flames.

'All right,' she said in a voice that was barely audible. 'Pete told me.' She paused. 'You can't be serious.'

'I am serious, Diane.'

'I don't believe you.'

'I'm not paying. Start believing it, Diane. I'm not paying.'

'You have to pay.'

'I don't have to do anything.'

'They asked *you* for the money.'

'Yes, a bunch of crooks asked. Why should they make the rules? Why should I play the game according to their rules?'

'Rules? Game? There's a little boy involved here.'

'There's a whole lot more than a little boy involved,' King said.

'There's nothing more than a little boy involved,' Diane answered. 'If you don't pay them, they'll kill him.'

'He may be dead already.'

'You can't even consider that possibility.'

'Why can't I? I can consider every damn aspect of this thing. I've been asked to pay five hundred thousand dollars for a boy who means absolutely nothing to me. I've got every right to weigh the possibilities. And one possibility is that he's already dead.'

'They told you he was still alive. You know they did. You can't excuse yourself by . . .'

'And another possibility is that they'll kill him even if I do pay. Ask the police. Go ahead. See what they—'

'And if you don't pay, they'll most *certainly* kill him.'

'Not necessarily.'

King rose from his chair. He left the fire reluctantly, walking to the bar unit at the other end of the room. 'Would you like a brandy?' he asked.

'No, I would not like a brandy,' She watched him as he poured. His hand was steady on the neck of the bottle. The amber fluid filled the brandy snifter. He recapped the bottle, walked back to the easy chair and gently rolled the glass in his big hands. She continued watching him, and finally she said, 'Doug, you have no right to gamble with Jeff's life.'

'No? Who has a better right? Who'd they ask for the money? What is Reynolds doing to get his son back? He's sitting on his behind, the way he's sat all his life. Why should I have to pay for *his* son?'

'Doug, I'm trying very hard to keep from screaming. I'm trying with all my might to keep from screaming.'

'Go ahead and scream if it'll make you feel any better. Actually, there's nothing to scream about. I shouldn't have been asked to pay, and I'm not paying, and that's that. It's a closed issue as far as I'm concerned.'

'But he's a child! A *child*!'

'I don't care what he is. He's nothing of mine.' He paused as if searching for a clincher to his argument and then said, 'I don't even *like* him, do you know that?'

'He's a child, damn you!'

'All right, he's a child. What's that got to do with it? Am I responsible for him? How is he my responsibility, child or adult, or creature from the depths? How the hell is he my responsibility?'

'They meant to take Bobby,' Diane said. 'That's what makes Jeff your respon—'

'Yes, but they *didn't* take him, did they? They goofed. They took Jeff.' King paused. 'Honey, when I was in the service and the guy standing next to me got killed, I didn't feel responsible for his death. I was simply tickled to death the bullet hadn't clipped me. I felt no guilt and no responsibility. I hadn't fired the rifle that discharged the bullet that killed him. My hands were clean. And they're clean now, too.'

'This is different,' Diane said. 'You're not so stupid that you can't see this is different.'

'I'm not stupid at all. How in the hell can I give them all that money? Don't you think I'd give it if I had it?'

'You *have* got it! Don't lie to me, Doug. For God's sake, don't pretend.'

'I need every cent I have for this deal. Seven hundred and fifty thousand dollars. How can I give away two thirds of that? Don't you understand?'

'Yes, I understand completely. A boy's life against a business deal.'

'No! A boy's life against *my* life!' King shouted.

'Doug, Doug, don't insult my intelligence! This wouldn't be the end for you. Don't say your "life" as if—'

'My life, my life!' King insisted. 'Just that! Everything I've worked for since as long as I can remember. This business is a part of me, Diane, don't you realize that?'

'The hell with the business,' she snapped. 'I don't care if you never own Granger Shoe! I simply don't care. If you owned Granger, if you owned United States Steel and got them by letting a boy die . . .'

'It's my life, my *life*!'

'And it's his death! Your life against his death!'

'Don't throw semantics at me,' King said angrily. He put his glass down on the coffee table and rose suddenly, beginning to pace the room. 'It's my death, too. What happens to me if I pay that ransom? I'll tell you what happens. Benjamin and his goddamn vultures will team up with the Old Man and kick me into the street. You were worried about what I did to Robinson, about his ever getting a job again. Okay, do you know what they'll do to *me*? My name'll be mud in the industry. A power grab that failed! Do you think any other firm would trust me after that? Do you think I'd ever get this far again? I'd be finished, Diane. Finished!'

'You could start again. You could—'

'Where? Where do I start? And how far do I go? Goddammit, even the office boys would watch me to make sure I never got too big again. I'd be chained to a desk. Is that what you want for me? Is that living?'

'Yes, it's living. There are hundreds of men chained to—'

'Not me! Never.' He paused. 'And what about yourself, Diane? Think of yourself. All this would go.' He gestured wildly with his hands. 'The house, the cars, the way we live, even the goddamn food we eat!'

'I'd choke!' Diane said. 'If you let Jeff die, I'd choke with every bite I took.'

'Then who's supposed to die? Me? Am I supposed to die for him? What is he to me?'

'He's a human being, that's all. Another human being. You used to care about . . .'

'All right, and I'm a human being, too. What the hell do I owe humanity, this great faceless mass named by the gentle spirits of our time? What has humanity, anonymous *humanity*, ever handed me? Nothing! I've clawed an existence for myself, clawed it out of solid rock until my hands are bleeding. How could you know, Diane, how could you possibly know? You were attending a private school while I was working my ass off in Granger's stockroom. I've worked for this business all my life, don't you see, all my life! And only because I could see into the future, the time when—'

'I don't want to hear it. If you mention the business

again, I'll . . . I'll punch you. I swear to God, I'll punch you!'

'All right, forget the business. Just tell me why *I* should pay. How many people out there have more money than I'll ever have. I'm poor, for God's sake. By comparison, I'm poor. It's taken me years to reach the point where I can afford this deal. There are people who make deals like this every day of the week, pick up a phone, close it by saying yes or no. Why haven't we had munificent offers from some of them? Why don't *they* pay the goddamn ransom?'

'That couple in Calm's Point offered you a thousand dollars, Doug. And they're probably poorer than you ever were.'

'Sure, a thousand dollars. What percentage of their life's savings is that? How much have they got in the bank *besides* that? Have they got five thousand? Okay, let's send them a return wire and ask for the entire sum, the entire five, not just the portion of it represented by the thousand they offered. Let's tell them they have to give us their life savings or a boy will die. What plans have they made for that money, Diane? A down payment on a house in the country? A new car? A trip to Europe? What? Ask *them* to give up their plans and their dreams for a kid who means nothing to them. Go ahead, ask them. Ask anybody in the world! Ask all of your sweet loving humanity! Ask humanity to commit suicide for a brother!'

'*You* were asked,' Diane said. 'You can't pass the buck.'

'I know I was asked, and I'm saying it's unfair. It's idiotic! I'm saying *nobody* should be asked.'

Diane sat at his feet suddenly. She took his hands in

her own and looked up into his face. 'Look,' she said gently, 'if . . . if Jeff were drowning and . . . and you were standing there on the shore . . . why, you'd automatically jump in after him, wouldn't you? You'd save him. That's all I'm asking of you now. Save him, Doug. Save him, please, please, pl—'

'But why me?' King said plaintively. 'Because I took the trouble to learn how to swim? Why didn't Reynolds learn to swim? Why should he come to me now and say, "Save my son! I never bothered to learn how to swim!"?'

'Are you blaming Reynolds for what happened?'

'Don't be silly, how could I?'

'For what then? For being a chauffeur? For not having five hundred thousand dollars?'

'Okay, I *have* got five hundred thousand, and I didn't get it by sitting around and watching the world go by. So where's the justice? I've worked hard for everything I've ever—'

'Reynolds has worked hard, too!'

'Not hard enough, then! Not half as hard! If he had, I wouldn't have to ransom his goddamn son! He's a sitter, Diane. And the sitters all want something for nothing. The big jackpot! The big country of quiz programmes that pay thousands of dollars for worthless information! Want a million dollars? Sure, go out and win it! Bull! Go out and work for it! Work like a bastard, until your fingers are—'

'Stop it, stop it,' she said.

'What is Reynolds saying to me? He's saying, "Help me, I'm helpless." Well, I don't want to help. I don't want to help anybody but myself.'

'You don't mean that,' Diane said, dropping his hands. 'You can't mean that.'

'I do mean it. Don't you think I'm tired too, Diane? Don't you think I'd like to *sit*?'

'I don't know what to think. I don't know anything about you any more.'

'You don't have to know anything about me. I'm a man fighting for his life. That's all you have to know.'

'And Jeff's life?' she asked, suddenly rising. 'Do you want them to kill him?'

'Of course I don't!' he shouted.

'Don't yell at me, Doug! They will kill him. You know they will!'

'I don't know they will! And it's not my problem. He's not mine. He's not my son!'

'He's there *because* of your son!' Diane shouted.

'I'm sorry about that, but it wasn't my—'

'You're *not* sorry! You don't care what they do to him. Oh, my God, you don't give a damn what happens to that—'

'That's not true, Diane. You know I . . .'

'What's happened to you, anyway?' she said. 'What's become of you? Where's Douglas King?'

'I don't know what you . . .'

'Maybe I shouldn't have stood by watching all these years, never raising a finger. Yes, you clawed, oh God, *how* you clawed your way, but I told myself this was an admirable trait, a desirable trait. This was a *man*, I told myself, the man I love. Even when I realized what you were doing to people, I excused it, I said it was simply your way. I convinced myself that you weren't cruel and ruthless and—'

'How does this make me ruthless? Isn't self-preservation more important than—'

'Shut up and listen to me!' Diane said. 'All those

years, God, all those years and this was what you were becoming! *This!* I watched when you crushed Di Angelo to get the cutting-room-foreman job, and I watched while you smashed half a dozen men in that factory to get to the top, and I watched while you ruined Robinson, and I was ready to watch on this Boston thing, knowing you'd throw the Old Man, *and* Benjamin, *and* how many others into the street! With resignations, Doug? Would you have allowed them to resign? Oh, God!' She covered her face with her hands, unwilling to sob, unwilling to show any sign of weakness.

'This is a different thing entirely,' King said.

'No, this is the same damn thing! The same pattern! Over and over and over again. People just don't mean anything to you any more, do they? You just don't care about anything but yourself!'

'That isn't true, Diane, and you know it. Haven't I always given you whatever you wanted? Haven't I been a good father to Bobby? A good husband to—'

'What have you ever given to me or Bobby? A roof? Food? Trinkets? What have you ever given of *yourself*, Doug? When have I ever meant more to you than your business? What am I now but a good bed companion?'

'Diane . . .'

'Admit it to yourself! You said the business was your life, and you meant it! Nothing else matters a damn to you! And now you're ready to murder a boy! After all these years, you've arrived! You're finally ready to murder an innocent little boy!'

'Murder, murder, you throw the word around as if—'

'It's murder! Pure and simple! You can call it what you want, but it's murder! You are about to commit a murder and, goddammit, this time I won't watch you do it!'

'What do you mean? What are you talking about?'

'I mean *this*, Doug. I mean you'll pay those kidnappers.'

'No. I won't, Diane. I can't.'

'You can, Doug, and you will. Because you're going to have to choose between your business and something besides Jeff's life.'

'What?'

'If you don't pay them, Doug, I'm leaving.'

'Leav—'

'I'm taking Bobby and I'm getting out of this house.'

'Now, come on, Diane, you don't know what you're saying. You're . . .'

'I know exactly what I'm saying, Doug. Pay those men, because I don't want to be anywhere near you if you don't! I don't want to be anywhere near something that's turned rotten and filthy.'

'Diane . . .'

'Rotten and filthy,' she repeated. 'Like one of the machines in your factory. A filth-clogged—'

'Honey, honey,' he said, and he reached out for her. 'Can't you—'

'Get away from me!' she shrieked, and she pulled away from his grasp. 'Not this time, Doug! This time you don't drag me into bed and make everything all right that way! I don't want your hands on me, Doug. This time you're doing murder, and I've had it – right up to here!'

'I can't pay,' he said. 'You can't ask me to.'

'I'm not asking, Doug,' she said coldly. 'I'm telling. When those men call tomorrow morning, you'd better have the money for them. It had better be ready and waiting for their instructions, Doug. It had better be.'

'I can't give it to them,' he said. 'Diane, I can't pay. You can't ask me to.'

But she had already walked out of the room.

10.

MORNING.

The city slumbers. The piercing cold is designed for late sleeping. It couples with the blackness outside to make the bed a sanctuary. There are cold floors in this city, and no one is anxious to touch them with bare feet.

The alarm clocks begin to ring when it is still dark. There is no sign of the sun as yet. The stars are beginning to flee the vault of night, but there is no spark of warmth on the horizon to the east. The morning is filled with blackness, and the alarm clocks penetrate the gloom with their staccato rings and persistent hums, their automatically tuned music, Good morning, America, it's time to rise and shine.

Go to hell, and the hands reach out to silence the never sleeping voices of time, go to hell, and a shoulder is turned into a warm blanket, flesh touches flesh, George, it's time to get up.

Mrmmbbb.

George, honey, it's time to get up.

The Georges of the city slip from beneath the blankets, leaving the warm womb of the connubial bed, their toes touching icy floors. The Georges of the city shiver and dress quickly, and the water in the tap (hot or cold, it makes no difference) all feels as if it is rushing from an icy mountain stream. It is a chore to shave. The light in the bathroom casts a cold eerie glow.

The wife and the kids are still asleep, and there is something unnatural about being the only person awake in the apartment, one of a million Georges who are awake throughout the city, performing their early-morning toilets. It is still cold in the apartment, but the radiators are beginning to bang now, and soon there will be the hiss of heat, the penetrating smell of heat. The coffee pot in the kitchen is beginning to perk, and the rich aroma of the brew will invade the apartment soon. Even the water from the tap feels a little warmer now. But best of all, the sun is coming up.

It rises without a problem. Boldly, it peers over the edge of the night, wearing a halo that turns the bowl of the sky upon itself, sends it rushing away, spikes of yellow intimidating the deep blue, fiery oranges boldly pushing at the night, rising, rising, like a giant suddenly standing, the sun touches the east, lines the edges of the building with sudden yellow, washes the River Harb in gold, covers the streets with warmth, no problems has the sun, no complexities, it is simply a matter of rising, it is simply a matter of shining. Good morning, America, it's time to rise and shine.

The neon lamps blink in sudden weakness against the overwhelming power of the sun. In the empty canyons of the city, the traffic signals click monotonously. There is no traffic; the reds and greens are meaningless. There are no pedestrians to heed the Walks and Don't Walks. Reds and greens flash, and the sun's single hot eye reflects on the countless glass eyes of the traffic signals, lights the windows of the tall buildings so that they gleam eastward with a hundred torrid glares.

A blind man taps his way along the pavement.

On the river, the traffic comes to life. The Georges of

the river wake to the smell of brine and cooking bacon. The whistles begin to hoot up and down the curving waterfront. On a Navy vessel, reveille is piped over the loudspeaker system.

The street lamps go out.

There is only the sun now.

A patrolman makes his silent rounds, trying the knobs of stores, leaning close to the plate-glass doors, peering into shops. He glances at his watch. Five-forty-five. In a few hours he will be relieved on post.

It has been a long, cold night.

But now it is morning.

She packed in the silence of the sun-washed bedroom. Dust motes climbed the shaft of sunshine, limning her figure as she methodically filled the bag. Liz Bellew watched her, sipping at a cup of coffee, curled up on the chaise longue alongside the bed.

'I haven't been up this early since the morning Alpha Beta Tau staged a panty raid,' Liz said.

'I remember,' Diane answered.

'Flaming youth, where have you gone? Alpha Beta Tau raided panties, and all Harold raids is the icebox.'

'We all have to grow up sometime, Liz,' Diane said. She opened one of the dresser drawers, removed a pile of slips from it and brought them to the bed.

'Do we?' Liz asked. 'And when do you grow up, honey? This seems like a pretty childish thing to me.'

'Does it?'

'Yes, it does. Unless you happen to have a suicidal urge.' Liz pulled a face and sipped at her coffee. 'But I always had you pegged as a pretty levelheaded girl. So now you're asking Doug to ruin himself and you besides. That doesn't make sense.'

'Doesn't it?'

'No.' Liz frowned. 'I wish you'd stop picking up the tail ends of my sentences and turning them into questions. It sounds a bit like imitation Hemingway.'

'I'm sorry.' Diane smoothed out a slip, folded it and put it into the bag. 'Suppose it were one of your children out there, Liz?'

'I'd cut off my arm to save him,' Liz answered unhesitatingly.

'And suppose it were my boy – Bobby – and they asked *you* for the money?'

Liz took a long pull at the coffee. It was still early morning, and she wore no make-up, but she was beautiful even without it, and her eyes were clear. 'Darling,' she said, 'I love you like a sister. Always have, and this isn't just a college-days-remembrance bit. But I'm not sure I'd part with five hundred thousand bucks to save your son. I'm just not sure, Diane. And if that makes me a bitch, so be it.'

'I'm surprised,' Diane said.

'Why? Because I'm a mother? I'm only a mother to the three little monsters who cavort through the house on the hill. I'm not a mother to all humanity, thank God.' Liz paused. 'Three pregnancies were enough.'

They were silent for a while. Liz finished her coffee and put down the empty cup. Diane continued packing.

'It was good of you to offer me a place, Liz,' she said.

'The least,' Liz said breezily. 'But if Doug asks me what I think about all this, I'll tell him quite frankly that you are nuts.'

'You needn't bother. He thinks so already.'

'Are you sure this kidnapping business is behind your leave-taking?' Liz asked. 'There's not something else? This is Aunt Lizzie, darling, so don't be afraid to—' She stopped suddenly. 'He's still good in bed, isn't he?'

'Yes, he's fine.'

'Then what the hell's wrong with you? Unpack that bag and go down and kiss him, for God's sake.'

'Liz,' Diane said calmly, 'he's *out* of bed sixteen hours a day.'

'Darling, we mustn't be greedy,' Liz said, lifting one eyebrow.

'Don't joke, Liz, please. This isn't fun for me.'

'I'm sorry.'

'He knocked on the door three times during the night,' Diane said. 'The last time, he sounded as if he was crying. Can you imagine Doug crying?' She paused. 'I wouldn't open the door for him. He's got to know I'm serious. He's got to know I'm leaving unless he pays that ransom.'

'Why don't you simply ask him to shoot himself in the head?' Liz said.

'I'm only asking him to do what any other human being would do.'

'Don't talk about human beings when you talk about tycoons,' Liz answered. 'They're a breed apart.'

'Then I want no part of the tycoon. If money and power are all that matter in life . . .'

'That's only a small part of it,' Liz said. 'Tycoonery is a disease. We laymen call it ants in the pants. Men like Doug and Harold couldn't sit still if you nailed them to the chair. They've got to be moving, they've got to be *doing* something. Render them inactive, and you're draining their life's blood.'

'And does "tycoonery" include the loss of all pity and

compassion for your fellow men?' Diane asked. 'Does it include all that, Liz?'

A knock sounded on the bedroom door.

'Who is it?' Diane asked.

'Me. Pete.'

'Would you get that, Liz?'

Liz Bellew uncurled herself from the lounge and went to the door. Opening it, she said, 'Good morning,' and Cameron looked at her in surprise.

'Liz,' he said. 'Didn't expect you here. Didn't even know you got up so early in the morning.'

'I always wake up early,' Liz answered. 'And always refreshed. How'd you sleep, Mr Cameron?'

'Fine, Mrs Bellew. Considering.'

'Then you haven't reached tycoon status yet. When you do, you'll begin scheming at night, too.'

Cameron smiled. 'I do all my scheming during the day, Liz.'

'Mmm, I'll bet you do,' she answered. 'And all your best work at night.' Their eyes locked. Diane, packing the bag, did not seem to notice. 'What brings you to the lady's boudoir?' Liz asked.

'A problem. I've got Doug's cheque in my pocket, Diane. What do I do? Go up to Boston with it? Or tear it up?'

'You'll have to ask him.'

'I ought to tear it up,' Cameron said. 'He's going to pay that ransom. I'm sure of it.'

'What makes you so sure?'

'He has to, don't you see?'

'No, I'm afraid I don't.'

'Well, look, let's say I go to Boston to close this deal, right? Douglas King then gets control of Granger Shoe.

But the newspapers'll smear him from here to China and back. Douglas King, they'll say, the man who now controls Granger Shoe, the man who refused to save a little boy's life. Hell, the publicity will ruin him. Do you think anybody would buy a pair of Granger shoes after that?'

'No, I don't suppose so. I hadn't thought of it that way.'

'Sure,' Cameron said. 'And you can bet Doug is considering that angle of it right now. That's why I'm certain he'll pay.'

'If that were his only reason for paying—' Diane started.

'What time did they say they'd call?' Liz interrupted.

'The kidnappers? They didn't say.'

Liz shook her head. 'And when they call, they ask the big question. I think the television quiz shows are more humane, don't you? At least they give you a week to decide.'

There was a cough at the door to the bedroom. They all turned. Douglas King stood there in robe and pyjamas. He was unshaven and his eyes were rimmed with red, but there was a cold deadly purposefulness to his stance. He stood in the doorframe like a spectre suddenly materialized. He issued his single cough and then said nothing, simply standing there and staring into the room.

'Good morning, Doug,' Cameron said. 'Sleep well?'

'No, I didn't sleep well.'

'God, you look awful, Doug,' Liz said.

'I'm supposed to look awful, didn't you know? My sins are all catching up with me. I'm a cruel, heartless bastard, that's me,' King paused. 'What are you doing here so early?'

'I called her last night, Doug,' Diane said. 'I'm taking Bobby there.'

'All ready for the big Sinking Ship scene, huh? Women and children first.' He turned to Cameron. 'When are you leaving, Pete?'

'What?'

'I said when are you leaving?'

'Well, I . . . I don't know.'

'What do you mean, you don't know? What plane are you on?'

'I didn't make a reservation,' Cameron said.

'Why not?'

'I thought . . .'

'It's not your job to think. I told you to get a reservation, didn't I? I gave you a cheque to deliver, didn't I?'

'Yes, but . . . I didn't know whether you still wanted me to.'

'Nothing's changed. Get downstairs and call the airport.' Cameron nodded and left the room.

Resignedly, Diane said, 'I guess I'd better finish packing, Liz.'

King stared at her for a moment and then went out of the room and downstairs. Cameron was already on the telephone.

'Eastern Airlines, please,' he said. 'Hello? I'd like to make a reservation for your first available flight to Boston. This morning.' He paused. 'Yes. This morning. Yes, I'll wait.' He cupped the mouthpiece and turned to King. 'They're checking it, Doug.'

'You should have taken care of this last night.'

'You going to let them kill that boy, Doug?' King opened his mouth, ready to answer, and Cameron turned back to the phone. 'Hello? Yes? Twelve noon? Hold on a minute, will you?' He cupped the mouthpiece again. 'Earliest flight is twelve noon. The others are filled.'

'Book it,' King said.

'All right, would you list me, please?' Cameron said into the phone. 'Mr Peter Cameron. That's C as in Charlie, a-m-e-r-o-n. Cameron. I've got a U-card, would you please – Yes, it's listed for Granger Shoe Company . . . . That's right, Granger with a G . . . . Check-in time is what? . . . All right, thank you.' He hung up and then turned to face King. 'Okay,' he said, 'we just chopped off Jeffry Reynolds's head.'

'Cut it out.'

'It's true, isn't it?'

'I said cut it out!'

'You are killing an eight-year-old boy, aren't you?'

'Yes, yes, I'm killing an eight-year-old boy – all right? I drink the blood of infants – all right? Don't you like what I'm doing? If you don't, pack your bag with the rest and get the hell out!'

'Now hold it a minute, Doug. There's no reason to—'

'I don't need any reason for anything! I'm just a ruthless, filth-clogged machine, and if you don't like my smell, you can leave with the rest of them!'

'Well, I guess that's putting it pretty plainly.'

'That's putting it pretty goddamn plainly, if you ask me. Make up your mind.'

'I still say it's murder,' Cameron said.

'Okay. If you think so, fine. I don't need men around me who—'

'Doug, listen to me. If our relationship has ever meant anything to you, for God's sake listen to me! Let the deal go! Save that kid! He's a young, defenceless child! You can't just . . .'

'When did you start loving young, defenceless children?'

'Aw, Doug, everybody loves kids! God, you can't be that—'

'And especially Pete Cameron, huh? The big child-lover. Don't you know this Boston deal will help you, too? Surely you know that, Pete. Hasn't any of my cold-hearted business acumen rubbed off on you after all these years?'

'Sure, I know it. But . . .'

'But it doesn't matter, huh? You love kids that much, do you? You love little runny-nosed Jeff Reynolds so much that Pete Cameron's career doesn't matter. Well, that's interesting. That's pretty damn interesting.'

'I'm not saying he matters more than my career, Doug. I'm saying . . .'

'Just what the hell *are* you saying?' Doug shouted, and the room went silent.

'Well . . .'

'Well?'

'I'm saying a boy's life is important.'

'But more important than this deal, right?'

'No, not more important, but . . .'

'More important or less important? Which?'

'Well, when you put it that way, I suppose . . .'

'If I pay the ransom, the deal falls flat on its face.

Now do you want the deal to collapse, or don't you? What's the matter, Pete? I've never seen you tongue-tied before. Does murder startle you?'

'No, no, it's just that . . .'

'Do you want this deal to fold, or don't you? Answer me.'

'No, I don't,' Cameron said.

'Then why are you so interested in the welfare of Jeffry Reynolds? When did you get so fatherly, Pete? I'm wondering when you got so ninety-nine per cent paternal?'

'It's for the boy,' Cameron said. 'How can we stand by and let a young defenceless—'

'If you give me that young, defenceless child crap again, I'll puke! What is it, Pete? What's the real reason?' King paused. A crafty glint touched his eyes. 'You got something of your own cooking? Is that it?'

'What? Me? Someth—Me?'

'Well, now,' King said. He moved a little closer to Cameron, a cold smile twisting his mouth. '*Well*, now. Now we're getting close, huh? Now we're . . .'

'Doug, don't be silly.'

'Why'd you call Benjamin yesterday? And never mind the Far Eastern Brocade baloney! What are you planning with him?'

'Me? Nothing. Doug, don't be ridiculous. I wouldn't plan anything with Benjamin.'

'Who *would* you plan something with?'

'Nobody.' Cameron laughed feebly. 'Nobody, Doug.'

'Did you tell Benjamin about this Boston deal?'

'Boston? Why, no. No.'

'Then why'd you call him?'

'About the Far Eastern Brocade line. I told you, Doug. The sales meeting . . .'

'Your secretary could have handled that! Why'd you make a personal call to Benjamin's house?'

'I . . . I wanted to tell him personally. I thought he'd be offended if I . . .'

'Yeah? Go ahead.'

'I . . . I just thought he'd be offended, that's all.'

King stared at Cameron silently for several moments. Then he went directly to the telephone and began dialling.

'What are you doing?' Cameron asked.

King did not answer. He stood with the phone to his ear, facing Cameron, waiting.

'The Benjamin residence,' a voice said.

'Get me Mr Benjamin,' King said.

'Who's calling, please?'

'Douglas King.'

'One moment, Mr King.'

'Why are you calling *him?*' Cameron said. 'I told you . . .'

'Hello?' a voice on the other end asked.

'George?' King said sweetly. 'This is Doug.'

'What is it, Doug?' Benjamin answered.

'How are you, George?'

'I'm fine. It's a little early in the morning, isn't it, to be exchanging—'

'George, I've been giving your proposition a lot of thought.' King continued staring at Cameron, who sat poised on the edge of his chair.

'Have you?' Benjamin said.

'Yes. It doesn't sound half bad to me.'

'Oh, doesn't it?' Benjamin said smugly. 'Well, well.'

'I'm thinking I may throw in with you, George.'

'Oh, you may, hey?'

'Yes. After all, there's more than myself to think about. There're a lot of other people who've served me loyally over the years. This would mean a lot to them, too.'

'You're such a Good Samaritan, Doug.'

'Well, I know I behaved badly yesterday, but, as I say, I've been doing a lot of thinking. Refusing your offer would simply be unfair to the people around me.'

'You should have done your thinking a little earlier, Doug,' Benjamin said triumphantly. 'You should have done your thinking before this kidnapping fouled up your deal in Boston!'

King's face changed. Studying Cameron, his mouth lengthened into a tight hard line and his eyes turned suddenly cold. 'My deal in Boston?' he repeated, and Cameron stiffened.

'Yes, yes, I know all about it, so don't get innocent with me,' Benjamin said.

'Well, that was just . . .'

That was just something that happened to fall through! Well, it's too damn bad, Mr King, but you played your cards and you played them wrong. My offer has been withdrawn. In fact, you might start looking for another job. You're going to need one as soon as we can call a meeting.'

'I see,' King said softly.

'I hope you do.'

'I guess I know when I'm over a barrel, George. But I hope this won't affect your attitude toward any of the people who've worked closely with me. Believe me, Pete knew nothing about what I was planning. I'd hate to see him pay for my errors. He's a good worker, George, and a bright—'

'Don't you worry about Pete!' Benjamin said, laughing. 'We'll take care of him.'

'You're not going to fire him, are you?'

'*Fire* him?' Benjamin's laughter grew louder. '*Fire* him? Fire your trusted, loyal assistant? Don't be ridiculous, Doug.' The laughter trailed off. 'If you don't mind, I'm late for the links now. Goodbye, Doug.' There was a click on the line. Slowly, King put down the phone.

'You son of a bitch,' he said to Cameron.

'Yes.'

'You told him about Boston.'

'Yes.'

'You gave him everything.'

'Yes.'

'Everything, you son of a bitch!'

'Yes, yes!' Cameron said, rising from his chair with nothing to lose now, exploding with a vengeance. 'Yes, I told him everything! And now you're going *out*! Out!'

'Oh, that's what you think, sweetheart!'

That's what I know, sweetheart. Benjamin's got the Old Man on his team now. You're going out, Mr King, and *I'm* going in. Me! Take a good look. Me!'

'I'm looking, you son of a bitch!'

'Look long and look hard! The next look you get is from the bottom of the heap!

'I'm looking! I'm looking, you miserable . . .'

'No more miserable than you, pal. I learned in your school. Did you expect me to bow and scrape forever? Did you expect Pete Cameron to be an assistant bottle washer for the rest of his life? Not me, pal. I learned. I learned fast!'

'Oh, you learned! I ought to strangle you, you bastard!'

'Why? What do you see, Doug? Yourself? Yourself ten years ago?'

'Myself ten—'

Take another look. I'm not you ten years ago. I'm you tomorrow! Tomorrow you're in the gutter. You're out, and I'm in. Tomorrow!'

'Not if this Boston thing goes through!'

'You haven't got the guts to kill that kid!'

'Haven't I? But you have, huh, Pete? Then why not me? We're alike, aren't we? The same school, no? Blood brothers, no? Both sons of bitches, no?'

He suddenly seized Cameron by the lapels of his suit and flung him across the room.

'Get out of my house!' he yelled.

'With pleasure, Mr—'

'Get out! Get out!'

Cameron went to the closet and quickly pulled his coat from a hanger. He reached into his trouser pocket, took out King's cheque, crumpled it into a ball, and threw it across the room.

'Get out!' King screamed. 'Get out, get out, *get out*!' The door slammed on his words, and still he shouted, '*Get out, get out, get out!*'

11.

THE BOY WAS cold.

She had given him her overcoat, but he still complained of the cold in the draughty farmhouse. He wanted cocoa, he said, something hot to drink, but there was nothing but coffee and evaporated milk in the house, and the boy sat on the edge of the bed as the sun stained the winter sky, and he shivered visibly and contained the sobs he would not release.

The two street maps had been set up alongside the radio equipment, and the men arranged them now so that they were clearly visible and easily read. The first map was a detailed map of Isola with Smoke Rise and the King estate marked with a red circle. A red line was inked onto the streets leading from the estate, following a tortuous route crosstown and over to the Black Rock Span. Once over the bridge, the red line took to the highways that crisscrossed Sands Spit, proceeding past a spot marked with a blue star, and then continuing out to the farthest tip of the peninsula. There did not seem to be much direction to the aimless meanderings of the inked red line. It moved from Smoke Rise erratically and then swooped toward the bridge with the precision of an arrow, only to assume an erratic course again once it hit the Sands Spit highways. The red line continued to reel drunkenly until it had passed the spot marked with the blue star, after which it again straightened, rushing with direct purposefulness toward the ocean. Perhaps significantly, it steered a wide course around a dot on the map which was marked simply 'Farm.'

Sitting with her arms around the shivering boy, Kathy tried to make some sense out of the maps, the radio equipment, and the snatches of conversation she overheard between Sy and her husband. The radio equipment was a necessary part of their plan, she knew, but she could not understand how they hoped to utilize it. The maps, too, were important, but again she could forge no connecting link between the radio and the maps set up near the chair in front of the equipment. The radio equipment included the oscillators and the transmitter Sy had mentioned, in addition to a microphone, and a dial which seemed far removed from any radio equipment she had ever seen.

She knew from the conversation that another phone call to King was in order, this one to ascertain that he had the money and to give him instructions about its delivery. After that, she knew, Sy was going to leave the house in the car while Eddie remained behind. More than that she did not know.

The boy trembled in her arms, and she held him close, and she wondered for perhaps the fiftieth time how the man she loved could possibly have become involved in a crime she considered heinous. The word 'heinous' did not enter her mind; it wasn't even a part of her vocabulary. But she considered kidnapping something unspeakably horrible, something almost inhuman, and she wondered what it was in Eddie, what drive, what lust for money, what search for identity, that could have led him into this final shattering act. It was her fault, of course. She knew that instantly. She knew with the intuition of a Cleopatra detaining an Antony, a Helen launching the Trojan war. The affairs of men were governed by women. This she knew, as all women know, with infallible instinct. And if Eddie had taken part in a kidnapping, was *now* taking part in the final stages of the theft of a child, then she was in part responsible for it.

She recognized in her own attitude about crime a peculiar dichotomy. She had, for example, sanctioned yesterday's excursion because she presumed Eddie and Sy were going out to rob a bank. The concept was almost amusing. In the hands of skilled players, it could indeed become a hilarious satirical sketch. 'Is this what you do to me?' the actress gun moll complains to the returning actor gangster. 'After I've given you the best years of my life? You go out to rob a bank, and you bring home a kid instead?' Very funny. Ha-ha. It was not humorous to Kathy, because it happened to be true in her case. Believing he was about to rob a bank, she had in effect given him her blessings. Confronted with a kidnapping instead, she heaped upon him her scorn.

Nor could she honestly say that she had exercised a great deal of effort over the years in pulling her husband away from crime. He had been in trouble as a youth, had been sent to reform school, where, under the skilled tutelage of tougher, more experienced youths, he had learned tricks he had never dreamed of. She hadn't met him until he was twenty-six, and by that time crime was as much a part of Eddie Folsom as his kidney. Was it this about him which had first attracted her? This attitude of nonconformity carried to its furthest extreme? This anti-social outlook which made the beatniks seem like members of a British soccer team? Perhaps, but she did not really believe so.

Eddie Folsom, in the eyes of Kathy Folsom, his wife, was not a crook. It is probably difficult to understand that because the good-guy/bad-guy concept is a part of our heredity, drummed into our minds together with the knight-on-a-white-charger ideal, and the only-bad-girls-lay taboo, and the slit-dresses-are-sexy fetish. There are good guys and bad guys, dammit, we all know that. Sure. But does the bad guy ever think of himself as a bad guy? When a gangster watches a gangster movie, does he identify with the police or with Humphrey Bogart?

Eddie Folsom, you see, was a man.

Short and simple, sweet and easily understood. Man. M-a-n. Kathy knew him as a man, and loved him as a man, and thought of him as a man who earned his living through stealing. But this did not make him a crook. True, Kathy knew the difference between right and wrong, between law and anarchy, between good and evil. But this did not make her husband a crook. A crook was the man at the butcher shop who thumbed the scale when weighing out lamb chops. A crook was the cab driver who had shortchanged Kathy in Philadelphia once. Crooks were people in charge of labour unions. Crooks were hired killers. Crooks were men who ran huge corporations.

And, unfortunately, crooks were people who planned and executed kidnappings.

And perhaps this was why the job disturbed her so much. In a single day, in the space of several hours, Eddie Folsom had stopped being a person who earned his living by stealing and had begun being a crook. And if this were the end product, if a person as sweet and as kind and as full of love as Eddie could turn into a crook, was not his wife to blame? And if she was to blame, where along the line had she compromised the ideal? Where had the good-guy/bad-guy concept ceased to have any real meaning? When had she decided that stealing was not a crime? It simply wasn't the kind of life she wanted for her man.

Wasn't this why she wanted to go to Mexico? So that Eddie could stop stealing, so that he could have his radio and do with it what he wanted, so that the demands of everyday living – simple things like wanting to eat, and wanting to be warm, and wanting a roof over one's head – could be satisfied with a maximum of security and a minimum of cold hard cash? A bank job, a last-time big splash. No more hiding, no more running. Mexico, and sun-washed streets, and skies as blue as Monday morning. Safety. Wasn't this all she really wanted for herself and her man?

Now, clutching a shivering eight-year-old boy to her bosom, Kathy Folsom felt something she had never in her life felt before. Holding a boy who was not her own, listening to the whispered plans of the men across the room, she wanted more than safety. She wanted the good to return and the bad to be over with. The trembling of the boy touched something deep inside her, a well-spring as old as Eve. She knew in that instant that the good-guy/bad-guy fiction was a legend designed not to fool but to inspire. And she knew why she was at fault in leading Eddie into his current dilemma. There was good in her man, a great deal of good. She had done a disservice to the good by casually accepting the evil. What she wanted to voice now was something spouted by every thief in every Grade-B melodrama. What she wanted to cry now were the words that poured from the mouth of the gangster as he lay bleeding in the gutter. What she wanted to sob out was the criminal's straight-man dialogue designed as a setup for Jack Webb's devastating closing punch line.

'Give me a break, will you?'

In the movies, the thief is instantly manacled and dragged bleeding to jail. On the television screen, the thief's eyes are wide with pleading. 'Give me a break, will you? Please. Give me a break.' And the taciturn spokesman for the Los Angeles Police Department answers, 'Did you give *him* one?'

There are no punch lines in real life.

Kathy Folsom wanted a break, a lousy break, another chance.

And she knew with intuitive female logic that many more lives than Jeff Reynolds's depended on the outcome of this job.

'Eddie,' she said.

He turned from the transmitter. 'What is it, hon?'

'The boy's still cold.'

'Who cares?' Sy said. 'What the hell are we running here? A nursery school?'

'He needs something hot to drink,' Kathy said. 'Would you go for something, Eddie?'

'I will never – never in my life – understand dames!' Sy said, an amazed expression on his face. 'The nearest store is maybe ten miles from here, and God alone knows how many cops are roaming the highways, and you want to send him out for a hot drink? That takes the prize, Kathy!'

'Will you, Eddie?'

'I don't know. I mean . . .'

'One of you has to go out to make the call, anyway,' Kathy said.

'Ahh, she's been listening. That's right, one of us does have to go out. But if it's me, I ain't running into any grocery store to buy something we can heat up.' He paused. 'And you're not either, Eddie. There's too much risk involved.'

'There's more risk involved if the boy gets sick,' Kathy said.

'Once we get the dough, we're never going to see this kid again, anyway,' Sy said.

'What do you mean?'

'Don't get excited! I meant we're leaving him here. You're going to Mexico, I don't know where the hell I'm going. So who cares if he gets sick?'

'It may be a while before they get to him,' Kathy said. 'If he got sick . . . if something happened to him . . .'

'She has a point, Sy,' Eddie said. 'Why make things tougher for ourselves? Look at the kid. He's shaking.'

' 'Cause he's scared.'

'I'm not scared,' Jeff said in a small voice.

'Won't you have to go to that store to make the call, anyway?' Kathy said.

'Yeah, but . . .'

'Won't it seem less conspicuous if you went in to buy something, and then just *happened* to make the call?'

Sy studied her with disgruntled admiration. 'That's not a bad idea,' he said. 'What do you think, Eddie?'

'I think so.'

'Okay. When you make the call, get the kid what he needs.'

'I'm going?' Eddie asked.

'Why not?'

'No, no reason. I'll go.'

'You know what to do? Find out if he's got the loot first. Then tell him to leave the house at' – Sy studied his watch – 'ten o'clock on the button. Tell him to go straight to his car, the Caddy with the DK-74 license plate – make sure you specify, Eddie. We don't want him using the wrong car. He's just liable to use his wife's Thunderbird.'

'All right,' Eddie said.

'So specify the Caddy. Tell him to go straight to the car and begin driving away from Smoke Rise. Tell him he'll be met by someone with further instructions. Make sure you say he'll be *met*.'

'Who's going to do the meeting?' Kathy asked. 'You?'

'Nobody,' Sy said, and he grinned. 'Tell him he'll be watched every step of the way and if he's followed by the police, we'll kill the boy. That's it. Then hurry back here. It's only eight now, and it shouldn't take you more than forty minutes or so to get to the store, make the call and come back. That gives us plenty of time.'

'Okay,' Eddie said. 'What do you want me to get, Kathy?' He went to the closet and put on his coat.

'A package of hot chocolate and some milk. Get some cookies, too, or some cupcakes. Whatever they have.'

He went to her and kissed her on the cheek. 'I'll be back soon.'

'Be careful.'

'Good luck, kid,' Sy said.

Eddie started for the door and then stopped. 'King's number.'

'Oh, yeah.' Sy opened his wallet and handed Eddie a scrap of paper. 'That the right one?' he asked.

'Yeah,' Eddie said.

'Can you read my Chinky handwriting?'

'Yeah.'

'Okay, take off.'

Eddie went to Kathy again, and again he kissed her on the cheek, and again she said, 'Be careful.'

Sy unlocked the door for him, and he went out of the house. They heard his footsteps on the gravel in the front yard, and then the sound of a car door slamming, and then the car starting. Sy waited until the car pulled out of the yard, waited until he could no longer hear the engine.

Then, locking the door again, he grinned and said, 'Well, well, alone at last.'

There were memories Steve Carella carried like heavy stones in his mind. There were things connected with police work which he would never forget, which would lurk always at the back of his skull, waiting to be called up fresh and painfully clear. He knew that the image of Charles Reynolds talking with Douglas King would become one of those memories, and even as he watched the man he wanted to leave the room, wanted to get away from the scene before it registered on his unconscious, before it joined the other lurking shapes.

He would never forget the smell of whisky in the liquor shop on the night he investigated the murder of Annie Boone, the broken trail of bottles, the girl's body pressed lifelessly to the wooden floor, her red hair afloat in alcohol.

He would never forget the moment of shocked surprise when he faced a boy with a gun, a boy he was certain would not shoot, and suddenly realized there'd been a lance of fire and an explosion, suddenly realized there was pain engulfing his chest, suddenly realized the boy had indeed pulled the trigger, the ground going out of focus, falling, falling, he would never forget that cold day in the park although he had already forgotten the name of the boy who had shot him.

He would never forget bursting into Teddy's apartment before she became his wife, confronting a killer who had literally been sent there by a reporter named Cliff Savage, firing low and firing fast before the man with the .45 could take a careful bead. He would never forget the scent, the feel of Teddy in his arms when it was all over. He would never forget these things.

And now, listening to Charles Reynolds, he wanted to plug up his ears, close his eyes, blot out what was happening, because he knew with certainty that the scene would haunt him for the rest of his life.

The man had come into the living room through the dining-room arch, standing hesitantly in the archway, waiting for Douglas King to notice him. King had been busy lighting a cigarette, his hands trembling slightly, and Carella had been sitting at the wiretap, watching King, and then suddenly aware that Reynolds was standing on the threshold to the room. There was on Reynolds's face a look of utter despair which, through contamination, infected his entire body. His shoulders were slumped, and his hands hung limply at his sides. Patiently, lifelessly, he stood in the doorway, waiting for King to turn, waiting for the owner of the house, his employer, to notice him.

King walked away from the coffee table, blew out an impatient stream of smoke, said, 'They probably won't even call—' and noticed Reynolds. He pulled up short, sucked in on the cigarette again, and said, 'You startled me, Reynolds.'

'I'm sorry, sir,' Reynolds paused. 'Sir, I . . . I would like to talk to you.' He paused again. 'Mr King, I would like to talk to you,' and Carella knew from those first words that this was going to be painful, and he wanted to get out of the room.

'Reynolds, couldn't . . .' King started, and then hesitated. 'All right, what is it? What do you want, Reynolds?'

Reynolds took a single step into the room, as if that was as far as he was prepared to go, as if even that single step was a break of the rules he had formulated for himself before making his entrance. His shoulders slumped, his hands hanging awkwardly, he said, 'I want to ask you to pay the ransom for my son, Mr King.'

'Don't ask me,' King said, and he turned away.

'I'm asking you, Mr King,' Reynolds said, and he extended his hand as if to pull the retreating King closer to him. But he did not budge from his spot just inside the entrance archway. He stood with his hand extended and pleading, until King turned to face him again from the other end of the room. And then, separated by forty feet of living-room area, separated by God alone knew how many miles, the two men faced each other like knights about to charge with lances, and Carella felt like a spectator who had no favourite.

'I have to ask you, Mr King,' Reynolds said. 'You see that, don't you?'

'No. No, I don't. Please, Reynolds, I really feel . . .'

'I have never begged in my life,' Reynolds said awkwardly, 'but I'm begging you now. Please, Mr King. Please get my son back.'

'I don't want to listen,' King said.

'You have to listen, Mr King. I'm talking to you like a man now. A father to a father. I'm pleading with you to save my son. God, God, please save my son!'

'You're coming to the wrong person, Reynolds! I can't help you. I can't help Jeff.'

'I don't believe that, Mr King.'

'It's true.'

'I . . . I have no right. I know I have no right. But where else can I go? Who else can I turn to?'

'Do you know what you're asking me to do?' King said. 'You're asking me to ruin myself. Am I supposed to do that? Goddammit, Reynolds, I wouldn't ask that of *you*!'

'I *have* to ask!' Reynolds said. 'Is there a choice for me, Mr King? Is there someplace I can go, someplace to get five hundred thousand dollars? Where? Tell me. I'll go. I'll go. But where? No place.' He shook his head. 'I'm coming to you. I'm asking you. Please, please . . .'

'No!'

'What do you want me to do, Mr King? Name it. I'll do it. Anything you say. I'll work for the rest of my life, I'll . . . '

'Don't talk nonsense. What can you possibly . . . ?'

'Do you want me to get down on my knees, Mr King? Shall I get on my knees and beg you?'

He dropped to his knees, and Carella winced and

turned away. Separated by forty feet of broadloom, the men stared at each other, Reynolds on his knees, his hands clasped, King standing with one hand in the pocket of his robe, the other hand holding a trembling cigarette.

'Get up, for God's sake,' King said.

'I'm on my hands and knees, Mr King,' Reynolds said. 'I'm begging you. Begging you. Please, please, please . . .'

'Get up, get up!' King said, and his voice was close to breaking. 'Good God, man, can't you—'

'. . . save my son.'

'Reynolds, please.' King turned away, but not before Carella saw him squeeze his eyes shut tightly. 'Please, get up. Please, man. Please. Could you . . . could you leave me alone? Could you? Could you please do that? Please?'

Reynolds got to his feet. With great dignity, he dusted off the knees of his trousers. He did not say another word. He turned and walked stiffly out of the room.

Humiliated, Douglas King stared at the door.

'Does it make you feel like a big turd, Mr King?' Carella asked.

'Shut up!'

'It should. Because that's what you are.'

'Goddammit, Carella, I don't want to listen to—'

'Oh, go to hell, Mr King,' Carella said angrily. 'Just go to hell!'

'What's the matter with you, Steve?' Byrnes asked, coming down the steps. 'Let's cut that out.'

'I'm sorry,' Carella said.

'I was just on the phone upstairs,' Byrnes said. 'I

checked our list of stolen cars and, sure enough, there she was. A grey 1949 Ford. Teletype's going out on it now. I don't suppose the licence plate'll still be the same one as on that list, do you?'

'No, sir.'

'Now just cut it out, Steve,' Byrnes said.

'Cut what out, sir?'

'The slow burn.'

'I wasn't—'

'You were, and don't lie to me, and remember that we've got a job to do here, and we're not going to get it done if everybody goes around with his ass being—' He cut himself short. Liz Bellew was coming down the steps, one hand clutching a valise, the other holding Bobby King's hand.

'Good morning,' she said. 'Any word yet?'

'No, ma'am,' Byrnes said.

'Daddy?' Bobby said.

'What is it, son?'

'Is Jeff back yet?'

'No, son. He isn't.'

'I thought you were getting him back.'

There was a long uncomfortable silence. Carella watched them and devoutly hoped he would never see the look that was on Bobby King's face at this moment on the face of his son, Mark, in years to come.

'Bobby, you should never throw questions at a tycoon so early in the morning,' Liz said breezily. 'He's coming over to my house for now, Doug.' She winked. 'It'll work out.'

'Where's Diane?'

'Upstairs putting on the finishing touches.'

'Did you . . . ?'

'I talked to her.' Liz shook her head. 'It's no go. But give her time.' She turned to Byrnes. 'Do I get a police escort, Lieutenant?'

'Darn right you do.'

'Make it the tall redheaded cop,' Liz said. 'The one with the white streak in his hair.'

'Detective Hawes?'

'Is that his name? Yes, him.'

'I'll see if I can.'

'He's just outside the door, Lieutenant, getting some air. I saw him from the upstairs window. Shall I tell him his services are required?'

'Yes, yes,' Byrnes said, a look of puzzlement on his face. 'Yes, please tell him.'

'I shall tell him. Come along, Bobby, we're going to meet a handsome policeman.' She walked him toward the front door. At the door, Bobby turned.

'*Aren't* you getting him back, Dad?' he asked, and Liz pulled him through the open doorway and shouted, 'Yoo-hoo! Detective Hawes! Yoo-hoo!'

The door closed behind them.

'I feel I should make my position clear to you gentlemen,' King said, clearing his throat. 'I know that on the surface my refusal . . .'

The telephone rang.

King stopped speaking. Byrnes looked at Carella, and Carella rushed to the wiretap equipment.

'You'd better get on the trunk line, Pete!' he said, and Byrnes ran to the other phone and picked up the receiver, ready to speak.

'Go ahead, Mr King,' Carella said, 'answer it. If it's our man, keep him on the line.'

Over the ringing of the telephone, King said, 'What . . . what shall I tell him?'

'Just keep him talking. About anything. Keep him on the line.'

'And . . . the money?'

'Tell him you've got it,' Byrnes said.

'Pete . . .'

'It's our only chance, Steve. They've got to think we're playing ball with them.'

'Answer it, answer it!'

King hesitated a moment and then lifted the receiver. 'Hello?'

'Mr King?'

The voice was not the one King had heard before. A frown crossed his forehead. 'Yes, this is Mr King,' he said. 'Who's calling, please?'

'You know who's calling,' the voice said. 'Don't play dumb.'

'I'm sorry. I didn't recognize your voice,' King said, and he nodded to Byrnes, who instantly said into the trunk line phone, 'He's on the other wire now. Get moving.'

Sitting at the wiretap equipment with the headphones over his ears, Carella watched the spools of tape revolving as they recorded the conversation. Scarcely daring to breathe, he listened to the voice on the other end.

'Have you got the money, Mr King?'

'Well . . .'

'Yes or no? Have you got it?'

'Keep him talking,' Byrnes whispered.

'Yes, I have it. That is, I have most of it.'

'What do you mean, most of it? We told you . . .'

'Well, the rest should be here momentarily. You specified small bills, didn't you?'

'What's that got to do with it?'

'And no consecutive serial numbers. Five hundred thousand dollars is a lot of money, you know. And there wasn't much time. The remainder is being counted out at the bank now. It should be here within the half hour.'

'All right, fine. Now here's what you're to do. Do you have a wrist watch, Mr King?'

'Yes. Yes, I have one.'

'I want you to set it so that it's synchronized with mine. Take it off your wrist now.'

'All right. Just a moment.'

'Keep him talking,' Carella said. 'Keep him talking.'

'You got it, King?'

'Yes, I'm getting it.'

Into the trunk line phone, Byrnes said, 'What's happening there? For God's sake, I *told* you he was on the line!'

'How about it, King?' the voice asked impatiently.

'All right.'

'My watch says exactly eight-thirty-one. Set yours for the same time.'

'All right.'

'Did you set it?'

'Yes. I set it.'

'Fine. Now the rest I'm going to say fast and only once, so get it all the first time. You are to leave the house at ten o'clock sharp, and you are to be carrying the money in a plain carton. You will go straight to the garage, and you will get into the black Cadillac with the license tag DK-74. That is the car you will use, Mr King. Do you understand?'

'Yes, I understand,' King said.

'Hurry, hurry!' Byrnes whispered into his receiver.

'You will drive away from the house and away from Smoke Rise. You will be watched, Mr King, so don't attempt to take anyone in the car with you, and don't allow the police to follow you. If you are followed, we will kill the boy right away. Do you understand that?'

'Yes, I do. I have it.'

'Have they got it yet?' Carella whispered to Byrnes.

'The damn fools are . . .'

'You will continue driving, Mr King, until someone meets you with instructions. That's all you have to know for now. Leave the house at ten sharp, alone, *with* the money. Goodbye, Mr—'

'Wait!'

'Keep him talking,' Byrnes said. 'They've got it traced to Central on Sands Spit!'

'What is it, Mr King?'

'When do we get the boy back?'

'When we get the money, we'll call again.'

'How . . . how do we know he's still alive?'

'He's still alive.'

'Can I talk to him?'

'No. Goodbye, Mr King.'

'Wait! You . . .'

'He's gone!' Carella said, ripping off the headset.

'Son of a bitch!' Byrnes said. Into the phone, he shouted, 'He just hung up. How far have you . . . What? Oh. Oh, I see. Okay. Okay, thanks.' He hung up. 'Didn't matter a damn. He was using a dial phone. As soon as they traced it to Central, it got lost in the automatic equipment.' He turned to Carella. 'What'd he say, Steve?'

'A lot. Want me to play it back?'

'Yes, go ahead. Nice work, Mr King.'

'Thank you,' King said dully.

'His voice sounded different,' Carella said. 'Didn't you think so?'

'Yes,' King answered.

'I think we got a different customer this time,' Carella said. 'Mind if I start the playback with the previous call, Pete? Just to check the voices?'

'No, go right ahead.'

Carella looked at his watch. 'Eight-thirty-five. We've still got time,' he said, and he flipped the switch that reversed the tape.

It was eight-thirty-three when Eddie Folsom came out of the telephone booth. The ride to the grocery store had taken longer than Sy had estimated, but there was still nothing to worry about. It would be a long, long time before ten o'clock rolled around.

Casually, he walked to the counter.

'Let me have a package of hot chocolate,' he said, 'and a bottle of milk, and a box of those cookies there.'

12.

KATHY HAD BEGUN pacing at eight-thirty. Now, at eight-forty-five, she wandered the room aimlessly, the window facing the front yard serving as the focal point of her ramblings. She would walk to the window, lift the shade and look out at the front yard, draw the shade again, pace, wander, light a cigarette, and then end up back at the window again.

'Where is he?' she asked. 'Shouldn't he be back by now?'

'He'll be back,' Sy said. 'Relax.' He paused. 'He not only had to make the call, you know. He also had to do the daily marketing.'

'The boy . . .'

'The boy, the boy, the boy? I hear another word about the boy, I'm going to start a club for underprivileged kids! Man, am I sick to death of this job! I should have known better than to tie up with a jerk who runs out to buy milk!'

'He went out to make the call,' Kathy said. 'Someone had to do it.'

'He's also buying milk. And *hot chocolate*,' Sy said, using a falsetto on the words, giving them a mincing, oversweet quality.

'The boy is cold.' She glanced at Jeff where he lay huddled on the bed, Kathy's coat around him, a blanket over that. 'You're lucky he hasn't started crying.'

'You're lucky *I* haven't started crying,' Sy said. 'That money is so damn close I can taste it.'

'Sy, when Eddie comes back—'

'What time is it?'

Kathy looked at her watch. 'Eight-fifty. When he comes back, what are you going to do?'

'Nothing. Not until a little before ten.'

'And then what?'

'Stop worrying. Your milkman will return, and everything'll come off all right, and we'll be rich as hell. And you know why? Because Sy Barnard is handling this little shindig. If a small-time punk like Eddie was in charge—'

'He's not a small-time punk!'

'No? Okay, he's a big operator, okay? How'd you ever get involved with such a big operator, huh?'

'Oh, what do you care?'

Nervously, she walked to the dresser and opened her purse. Nervously, she began combing out her hair.

'I'm interested,' Sy said. 'Really.'

'We just met, that's all.'

'Where?'

'I don't remember.'

'The Safecrackers' Ball?'

'That's not funny, Sy.'

'But you knew he was in the rackets?'

'Yes, I knew. It didn't matter to me.' She paused. 'Eddie is good.'

'Yeah, he's a doll.'

'I'm not joking. Oh, why am I even talking to you!' She hurled the comb into her purse and then snapped it shut and walked to the window again.

'Didn't I say he was a doll?'

'He's in this because it's the only thing he knows,' Kathy said. 'But if he got away from it, if I helped him to get away from it, he'd be good. I know he would. I'd see to it.'

'Why'd you marry him?'

'I love him.'

'Warm for his form, huh?'

'When are you going to let me go?' Jeff said from the bed.

'Shut up, kid.'

'Aren't you ever?'

'I said shut up. I've had you up to here already!'

Kathy lifted the shade and scanned the yard again. Sighing, she turned away from the window.

'You worried about him?'

'Of course I am,' she said.

'What for? There's other fish in the ocean. Bigger fish. Smarter fish.'

'He's my husband.'

'Pull down the shade.'

'It's morning. Why can't . . . ?'

'I don't want nobody peeping in here.'

'There isn't a soul around for miles!'

'Pull it down!'

Kathy lowered the shade, walked to the dresser again, fished into her purse for a cigarette and, discovering she was out, snapped the bag shut angrily.

'Stop worrying,' Sy said. 'Husbands are for the birds. All they are is a piece of legal paper and a gold circle. Who the hell ever takes husbands seriously?'

'I do,' Kathy said. 'I love him.'

'Love is what they make up for teenagers. There ain't no such animal.'

'You're mistaken. You just don't know.'

'I know more than you think, baby, and about a lot of things. I know, for example, that your darling boy is rotten clean through. There ain't nothing you can do for him no more. It's too late now.'

'It's not too late. Once this is over . . .'

'Once this is over, there'll be another job, and another one after that, and then another and another and another! Who the hell are you kidding? Yourself? I seen bums like Eddie in prisons all over this country. He's rotten! He stinks! He's *me*, for Pete's sake! Do you think *I'm* such a prize?'

'I don't want to listen.'

'Okay, don't. The big reformer there. Gonna make a silk purse. Bullshit!'

'Don't talk like that, Sy. I don't . . .'

'Why? What are you gonna do about it?'

'I'll – Just don't talk like that.'

'You sound actually threatening, you know that? I got to watch my step, huh? Got to be careful. Not like little Blondie there, huh? He don't have to be careful.' Sy paused and then looked at the radio receiver. 'Eddie shoulda turned on the monster before he went out. We ain't heard nothing for a long while.'

'There's nothing to hear but the road blocks.'

'So? I find road blocks interesting.' He paused and studied her. 'Listen, you want a little drink?'

'So early in the morning?'

'Sure. Puts hair on your chest. Come on.'

'No.'

'What's the matter, baby? Don't you drink?'

'I drink.'

'So, come on, have one. For Pete's sake, we're sitting

on a fortune, you realize it? Are we supposed to mope around like a couple of corpses? What the hell is this, a graveyard? Come on, baby, loosen up.'

'If you want a drink, take one. Nobody's stopping you.'

'Right, baby! Nobody stops me from nothing I want!' He studied her speculatively for a moment, and then walked to the dresser. Picking up a pint bottle from its top, he held it aloft, said, 'Cheers,' and tilted it to his mouth. 'Good stuff. Change your mind?'

'I don't want any. Where's Eddie?'

'You getting nervous, huh?' He held the bottle out to Jeff. 'Want a slug, kid? Warm the cockles. No, huh?' He shrugged and wiped his mouth. 'You worry too much, Kathy. We could be having ourselves a real ball, insteada worrying. A real ball.' He smiled and nodded, staring at her. Kathy moved toward the window again, crossing her arms over the front of her sweater. 'You know what your trouble is, baby? You don't know how to live, that's what. You're all tensed up because darling hubby went to the grocery store. You got to learn to relax. Look at me. Cops covering the city like a plague. Do I worry? Hell, no.'

'How can I relax when Eddie may have run into trouble?'

'You can start by forgetting all about Eddie. Come on, have a little drink.'

'Oh, Sy, don't bother me! I don't want a drink.'

'Excuse *me*, I didn't know I was bothering you. Okay, stand around and worry if that's what you want to do. I can think of a lot better ways to kill the time, though.' He walked closer to her, his eyes on the front of her sweater. 'A dame like you should have good clothes, you know that? Where'd you get that crumby, moth-eaten sweater? Eddie should be ashamed of himself! You should be wearing fancy, lacy stuff. It ain't every dame can fill clothes like you.'

'I'm not interested.'

'What the hell's the matter now? For Pete's sake, I'm complimenting you!'

'Thanks,' she said dryly.

'Boy, there sure ain't no mutual-affection society here, is there? All the affection goes out to Blondie, don't it? Or Eddie, depending on who's around. But none to Sy, that's for sure. Well, you want to know what I think? I think you're wasting your time with a punk like Eddie, that's what I think. Best thing could happen to you is for the bulls to pick him up.'

'Shut up,' Kathy said.

'I'm shooting you the goods. Pretty little piece like you tied down to a second-rate punk. Who needs him? I can run this job alone. Honey, you're wasting your talents on him. What you need is somebody who knows the score, somebody who can—'

'Shut up, Sy!'

'Tell me the truth, ain't you hoping they pick him up? You was against this job to begin with, wasn't you? All you're worried about is little Blondie over there, will we hurt him, will we—'

'Shut up, *shut up*!'

'What is it? You got a yen for a family of your own? Is that it?' He laughed bitterly and tilted the bottle to his mouth again. Kathy walked to the window and raised the shade. Sy pulled the bottle from his mouth and shouted, 'Lower the goddamn shade!' She glared at him sullenly and then obeyed. 'Boy, this is some cheerful party, ain't it? Will I be glad when this gig is over. Man!' He held the bottle aloft in a toast. 'Here's to the object of the lady's affection, the dear little kidnap victim. Cheers, Blondie.' He drank. 'How about that, you little bastard? I just drank a toast to you.'

Jeff did not answer.

'I just toasted you,' Sy repeated. 'What's the matter, ain't you got no manners? Didn't your mother never teach you to say thanks? Or don't you know how to talk?'

'I know how to talk,' Jeff said. He was still trembling, both from the cold and from a very real fear which had begun the moment Eddie left the farmhouse.

'Then say something,' Sy said. 'The goddamn cops are chasing all over the city looking for me, and my partner is out marketing and I'm cooped up here with a frigid bitch, and on top of all that I drink a toast to your health, you little bastard. That's pretty damn white of me, I would say. How about a thank-you?'

'Thank you.'

'Or maybe you don't know the reason I'm cooped up here with Little Miss Cold Ass. Maybe you don't know *you're* the reason, huh? Or maybe you think I like this?' He paused. 'You know you're the cause of my misery?'

'I . . . Yes.'

'Oh, you know, huh?'

'Y-yes,' Jeff said, hugging the blanket to him.

'So what the hell're you gonna do about it?'

'Stop picking on the boy, Sy. And watch your language.'

'Stop picking on the boy, Sy, and watch your language,' he mimicked. 'Good to see that something gets a rise out of you, anyway. I was beginning to think maybe you had died and was already laid out.' He turned back to Jeff. 'I asked you a question, Blondie.'

'I . . . I don't know what to do about it.'

'Well, that's a hell of an attitude!' He paused. 'Isn't it?'

'Yes, I suppose . . .'

'Y-yes, sir.'

'One hell of an attitude, I would say. You're the cause of all my misery, and you don't know what to do about it. Well, how about thinking a little? A smart little bastard like you should be able to figure out something, don't you think?'

'Sy, leave him alone!'

'Yeah, and watch my language, I know. Well, you can go straight to hell, baby.'

'Why are you picking on the boy?'

'Who's picking on him? We're chatting. You want me to stop?'

'Yes.'

'Make it worth my while. Convince me.' Sy laughed and turned back to Jeff. 'Start thinking, kid. I'm waiting.'

'I don't know what you want me to say, sir.'

'I want you to come up with some ideas.'

'I haven't got any ideas, sir.'

'Well, now, ain't that a crying shame? No ideas. Tch, tch, tch. You just don't care what happens to me, is that it?'

'I . . . I don't know what to say, sir.'

'Say whatever the hell's in your head, stupid! When somebody asks you something, say what you think!'

'Y-yes, sir.'

'Okay. Would you like to see me get the electric chair?'

'I . . . I don't know.'

'*Sir!*'

'Sir,' Jeff said, beginning to get rattled. 'I don't know, sir.'

'You do know. Yes or no? Give me a yes or no answer. You want me to get the electric chair?'

'Sy, stop it!'

'Yes or no?' Sy persisted.

'Yes, sir. I . . .'

'What?'

'I would like to see you get . . .'

'What? What, you little bastard!'

'Sy, you're scaring him half to death! Can't you see?'

'You keep your ass out of this! Unless you've got some ideas!'

Jeff suddenly scrambled off the bed and rushed to where Kathy was standing, burying his head in her sweater, throwing his arms around her waist. Like a jealous suitor, Sy shouted, 'Get your hands off her!'

Kathy pulled the boy closer. 'That's enough, Sy.'

'What's enough? Who the hell are you – What the hell are you saying to me? You're telling *me*? There ain't a skirt alive who can tell *me* what to do!' He seized Jeff's arm and tore him away from her, flinging him across the room. 'There!' Sy said. 'How about that? How about that, you two-bit slut?' and Kathy slapped him with all the power of her arm, her shoulder, and her outstretched palm.

His hand flashed to his face. Slowly he lowered it. 'You want to play, huh?' He said. He reached into his pocket, and the knife came into view, the blade opening almost before it had cleared his pocket.

'You're finally ready to play, huh?' he said, and he swiped at her with the knife, forcing her to back away from him. He followed her across the room, slashing at her with the knife, not intending to cut her, simply toying with her, forcing her back until she collided with the door, and then he crouched before her with the knife swinging in front of his body in a wide arc.

'Sy, don't . . .'

'Don't what, baby? Don't cut you? Baby, would I cut you?' he said, and he lashed out with the razor-sharp blade, catching Kathy's sweater with the tip, drawing it away from her body, and then suddenly ripping upward with the knife, slashing the sweater up the front toward the neck.

'Sy!'

Again he slashed, using the knife with the precision of a duellist, ripping at the sweater, exposing her brassière. She tried to cross her arms over her breasts, but the knife flashed again, and she pulled her hands away from her body, the sweater hanging in tatters over the white brassière.

Sy grinned. 'Now the bra,' he said.

Her hands moved instantly, instinctively, to cover her breasts. He thrust out with the knife, and she pulled her hands back again, gasping uncontrollably now, waiting for the rip of steel that would sever the cotton bra.

'We're gonna let them beauties free,' Sy said, and he moved closer to her with the knife. 'Keep your hands down. I'd hate like hell to cut you! We're gonna let them big ripe . . .'

The boy seemed to materialize from nowhere. He landed on Sy's back with the ferocity of a wildcat, clawing, pummelling, punching, pulling at Sy's hair in a frenzy of unleashed anger. Sy straightened up, surprised, and then swung about and tried to shake the boy loose as Kathy ran for the door. He reached behind him for a grip, clutched at the boy's trousers and tore him loose, flinging him halfway across the room. Kathy, at the door, was fumbling with the lock. He reached her in two bounds, caught her arm, and pulled her to him, the knife tight in his right hand.

'Maybe you just better relax, baby,' he said. 'Maybe you'll like it better that—'

The three knocks sounded on the door. Leaning against the door as they were, Sy and Kathy recoiled sharply from the minor explosions against the wood.

'It's Eddie,' Kathy whispered, and she said the words like a prayer.

Sy backed away from her instantly. 'Put your coat on. Hurry up!'

She moved away from the door rapidly, took her coat from the bed, slipped into it and buttoned it to the throat.

'You mention a word of this to Eddie,' Sy said, 'and the kid is dead. You hear me? The kid is dead.'

Kathy nodded dumbly.

Sy went to the boy and sat beside him. 'Okay,' he said. 'Open it.'

Kathy stepped close to the door again. 'Eddie?' she said.

'Yeah. How about it? Open up, willya?'

She opened the door. He stepped into the room quickly, closing the door behind him and locking it.

'Jesus, what took you so—' he started, and then he saw Kathy's face and knew instantly that something was wrong.

'Welcome home, hero,' Sy said nonchalantly. 'You get the milk?'

'Yeah,' Eddie said. He carried his package to the table. Kathy began unpacking it silently. Eddie watched her. 'Hey, what's the matter here?' he said.

'Nothing,' Kathy said. 'Everything's fine, Eddie.'

'Kathy and I just had a little spat, that's all,' Sy said.

'What about?' Eddie asked. He looked at his wife again. 'What are you wearing a coat for?'

'I'm . . . It got chilly in here.'

'What'd you fight about?'

'She doesn't like the idea of the whole damn job,' Sy said. He shrugged. 'I shouldn'ta flown off the handle, I guess. I'm sorry, Eddie. You run into any trouble out there?'

'No. I didn't see a single cop the whole time I was on the road.' He looked at the pair suspiciously again. 'This is no time to be squabbling,' he said ineffectively. 'I mean, what the hell.'

'I said I was sorry,' Sy said.

'Yeah. Well.' Eddie shrugged.

'I'll make you some hot chocolate,' Kathy said to Jeff.

Tune in the monster, Eddie. Let's see what's happening out there.'

'What time is it?'

Sy looked at his watch. 'Little after nine. I should leave by about nine-thirty, just to make sure.'

'Yeah,' Eddie said from the receiver. He threw a switch and began tuning the set. 'I still don't know what you two had to fight about. We're almost near the end now, and you . . .'

'. . . *POSSIBLE LICENSE PLATE RN 6220. THAT'S . . .*'

'Jesus, lower that, will you?' Sy shouted over the sudden roar from the radio. Eddie quickly turned down the volume.

'. . . *a 1949 Ford sedan,grey,possible license plate RN 6210.*'

'Wh—?' Sy said.

'*Once more for the West Coast*,' the police dispatcher said. '*Car used in the Jeff Reynolds kidnapping may have been a 1949 Ford sedan, grey, possible license plate RN 6210 . . .*'

'They know the car!'

'Don't get excited!' Sy snapped.

'And I was driving it! Even with the changed plates, they could have—'

'Relax! For Pete's sake, don't panic!'

'They coulda picked me up. I coulda – Hey! How we gonna . . . ? Sy, the car figures in our plan. How we gonna use it now?'

'I don't know. Take it easy now.' Sy began pacing the room.

'What are we supposed to do? We can't let all that money go!'

'No. No. we can't. We won't have to. You said the roads were clear from here to the grocery store. Okay, chances are they don't have road blocks everywhere, how could they? Okay, that radio is gonna tell us just where they *do* have the road blocks! It's just a question of listening all over again, and taking down the information this time.'

'Sy, that don't sound safe!'

'What the hell are you worried about? It's me who'll be driving the car.'

'Still . . .'

Sy looked at his watch. 'We got about a half hour. Let's hope they give a lot during that time. Because whether they do or not, that car leaves here at nine-thirty. And you better be ready to do your share come ten o'clock.'

'Sy, if they get one of us, the whole damn job'll . . .'

'Don't you worry about me, kid,' Sy said. 'Nobody's gonna get this boy. Not when five hundred thousand bucks is riding on his back.'

'*. . . corner of Agatha and two-one-oh . . .*'

'Shhh,' Sy said.

'*. . . to relieve Car 108 in road block. You got that, 112?*'

'*This is 112. Roger.*'

'Good,' Sy said, nodding his head vigorously. 'Spiel it out, boy. Keep spieling it out.'

13.

AT TEN O'CLOCK in the morning, the front door of Douglas King's house opened. Douglas King, wearing a dark overcoat, black Homburg and pearl-grey gloves, stepped out of the house. He was carrying a brown carton stuffed with newspapers. He walked to the side of the house, looking briskly about him, went directly to the garage, pulled up the overhead door, entered the black Cadillac parked there and started the engine. He let the engine idle for several moments and then pulled the car out of the garage, executed a turn, and drove up the driveway to where the twin stone pillars flanked the road. He turned onto Smoke Rise Road and glanced into the rearview mirror. There was not a car or a person in sight. If anyone was watching his departure, that person was certainly well hidden.

He began driving aimlessly, going on a straight course for several blocks, turning off Smoke Rise Road and onto the viaduct over the River Highway, and then heading crosstown. No police cars were behind him. To the observer, Douglas King was following instructions to the letter. He had left the house at 10 A.M. carrying a plain carton full of money. He had got into his car alone and begun driving, awaiting further contact.

Any observer, casual or intent, could not possibly have known that Detective Steve Carella had entered the garage at 9.30 A.M. through the door leading from the kitchen, or that he had then climbed into the Cadillac and made himself comfortable on the floor in the back.

Lying there now, he said, 'Do you see anything?'

'What do you mean?' King answered.

'A car following us? A pedestrian signalling us? A helicopter hovering?'

'No. Nothing.'

'How the hell are they going to make contact?' Carella grumbled. 'Is God going to send down a thunderbolt?'

At ten o'clock in the morning, Eddie Folsom began warming up his radio equipment. Sy had left at nine-thirty with a list of road blocks clutched in his hand and embossed on his mind. Now, as the tubes glowed with life, as the hum of the oscillators and the transmitter filled the room, Eddie could feel a nervousness starting somewhere at the pit of his stomach and spreading through his body. He consulted his meters again, made sure he was on the right frequency, and then sat down before the equipment, the microphone set up directly before his face, the street maps not two feet from where he sat, the dial three inches from his right hand. He looked at his watch. It was ten-oh-three. He would give King another seven minutes. And then at ten-ten it would start.

'Anything yet?' Carella asked.

'No.'

'What time is it?'

'Ten-five.'

'Why'd you come along, Mr King?'

'That's my business.'

'You didn't have to. A detective could have taken your place.'

'I know.'

'Besides, I doubt very much that the house is being watched. Unless this gang is enormous, they couldn't possibly have that many . . .'

'Are you married, Mr Carella?'

'Yes.'

'Do you love your wife?'

'Yes.'

'I love mine, too. She walked out on me this morning. After all these years of marriage, she walked out on me. Do you know why?'

'I think so.'

'Sure. Because I wouldn't ransom Reynolds's boy,' King nodded his head, his eyes glued to the road. 'You think that's pretty rotten of me, too, don't you?'

'You won't win the Nobel Prize for it, Mr King.'

'Maybe not. But then, I don't want the Nobel Prize. All I want is Granger Shoe.'

'Then it shouldn't bother you that your wife walked out.'

'No, I guess it shouldn't. If Granger Shoe were all I wanted, I wouldn't care very much about Diane, or Bobby, or anybody, would I?'

'I guess not.'

'Then what am I doing here?'

'I asked first, Mr King.'

'I don't know what I'm doing here, Mr Carella. I only know this. I cannot pay that boy's ransom. I cannot because it would mean destroying myself, and that's impossible. I don't believe in fairy tales, do you?'

'No, I don't.'

'I'm what I am, Mr Carella. I don't think I'll ever change. Business is a part of my life and without it I might as well be dead. That's what I am. I make no apologies for it. And maybe I've been rotten, yes, maybe I have. And maybe I've hurt men, but I've never gone out to get anybody without a damn good reason, and that's what I am, and I make no apologies. It's taken me a long time to get where I am today, Mr Carella.'

'Where are you today, Mr King?'

'In a car, waiting for instructions from a thief.' King smiled thinly. 'You know what I mean. It's taken me a long time to get the things I always felt I needed. A man doesn't change, Mr Carella. Diane doesn't know what poverty is. How would she know? She's had money all her life. Not me, Mr Carella. I was dirt-poor. I was hungry. You don't forget poverty, and you don't forget hunger. I started working for Granger when I was sixteen. In the stockroom. I worked harder than the others. I stacked more damn shoes, and I carried more damn shoes, and I took pride in what was the cruddiest part of the plant because I knew that someday I was going to own that company. That sounds crazy, doesn't it?'

'Ambition never sounds crazy.'

'Well, maybe not. I learned that factory inside out and backwards. Every position, every phase, every person. I learned shoes. I learned shoes because this was going to be my company. It was going to be the only thing I ever knew or ever wanted. By the time I met Diane . . .'

'Where'd you meet her, Mr King?'

'I picked her up. The war was still on. World War Two, I mean.'

'Was there any other war?' Carella asked.

'I was in on furlough, a sergeant, a T-five. Were you in the Army?'

'Yes.'

'Then I don't have to explain how lonely your own home town can seem when you're home on furlough. I picked up Diane at the U.S.O. She was one of those rich girls doing their bit for the enlisted man. We danced together a few times. We clicked. Just like that. The rich girl from Stewart City had met the poor boy from Kelly's Corners and – Do you know the city well, Mr Carella?'

'Fairly.'

'Then you know the part familiarly referred to as Stewart City, hugging the river on the south of Isola, very fancy, doormen, penthouses, air conditioning. And you know where Kelly's Corners is, we used to call it Smelly Corners when I was a kid. We met, Mr Carella. Never the twain, but we met. And we clicked. And she married me. I went back to Granger after I was discharged. I was earning about sixty dollars a week for the first year of our marriage. That wasn't enough. Not enough for Diane, and not enough for me. So I began doing what had to be done. I began solidifying my position in that factory, and I stamped on anyone who got in my way because nothing had changed. I was still going to own it. I was going to make Diane Kessler's father eat his words. I was going to trudge up to his Stewart City apartment with the air conditioning and the mile-high carpeting and make him apologize to me for ever referring to me as a "worthless nobody." As a matter of fact, I never tasted that particular revenge. The old man died before I really got a toehold. And he died without asking for his daughter and never having spoken to her since that day we broke the news to him. I never had my revenge.'

'Revenge isn't sweet,' Carella said. 'It's only boring.'

'Sure, but I would have liked it. I know I would have. Five years later, I was ready to spit in his eye, but he was six feet underground, and you don't go to a man's grave to dance on it. Five years later, I bought the house in Smoke Rise. I wasn't quite ready for the house yet, but I knew the house would be important to me. And it was. A house is a wonderful bargaining tool, Mr Carella. You'd be surprised how many people in this world are impressed by the accoutrements of everyday living, the houses, the silverware, the cars – the window dressing. And now . . . here I am. I've still got the house, and I own or am about to own enough stock to make me president of Granger. My son goes to a private school, and I've got a cook, and a chauffeur, and a gardener, and a housemaid, and a sports car for my wife, and a Cadillac for me, and enough money to get whatever I want, Mr Carella. Whatever I want.'

'Then why are you here?' Carella asked. 'Why are you driving your own car waiting for contacts from men who may turn out to be worse than murderers?'

'I don't know. Or, yes, I do know. I can't give those men the money they want. I can't because it would kill me. If that makes me rotten, then all right, I'm rotten. But I can't change the way I am, Mr Carella. That's for the fairy tales. The mean witch who turns into a lovely princess, the toad who turns into a prince, the rotten louse who suddenly sees the error of his ways and vows to do good for the rest of his life, fairy tales, pap for the television viewers of America. I'll never change. I know it, and Diane knows it, and she'll come back to me, Mr Carella, because she loves me. I'll never change. And if I'm rotten, I'm rotten. But I've fought all my life, and if I can't give those men the money they want, I can fight them this way, by going along, by *doing* something.'

He shook his head.

'I know none of this makes any sense. For the first six months of my married life, we lived in an apartment that had cockroaches the size of flying bats. I never want that again, Mr Carella. I want my house in Smoke Rise, and I want my servants, and I want a Cadillac with a telephone hanging from the dashboard, and I want—'

And in that instant, the telephone hanging from the dashboard rang.

It had been a simple matter to learn the frequency band within which all automobile telephones in the vicinity operated. Once this had been learned, it was equally simple to steal the necessary equipment: the 600-volt oscillator and the 1600-volt oscillator, the transmitter and the various relays and switches, and lastly the batteries. It was a little more difficult to come across the dial which Kathy had thought seemed alien to a radio set – and only because it *was alien*. The dial was a telephone dial hooked to the battery and the relay, so that it could key the telephone in King's car and cause it to ring. Once King picked up the telephone, Eddie could speak to him over the microphone attached to his transmitter. King's automobile telephone number, quite naturally, had been obtained from the telephone company.

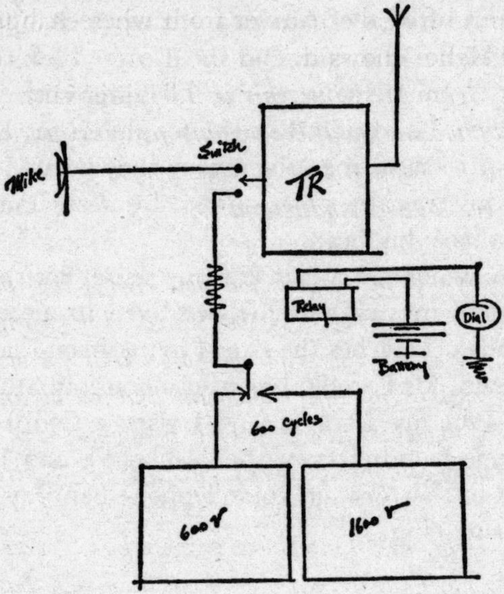

Eddie Folsom's preliminary sketches from the setup had looked like the diagram above.

The setup was now a reality before him. He had dialled King's number nervously. He waited now, one hand trembling around the microphone, the receiver tuned to pick up King's voice, the transmitter ready to relay Eddie's instructions.

Pick up the phone, he thought.

Pick it up!

'Wh—?' King said.

'What's—?' Carella said from the back seat.

'The telephone! The telephone's ringing.'

'Holy God, that's how – Answer it! Go ahead, answer it!' King lifted the receiver from where it hung on the dash. 'Hello?' he said.

'All right, Mr King, this is it,' Eddie said. *'You listen carefully, because you'll be receiving your instructions over this telephone for however long it takes you to get where we want you to go. Do you understand?'*

'Yes. Yes, I'm listening.'

'Nobody's going to help you now, Mr King, because this conversation can't possibly be traced. I'm using a radio transmitter and not a telephone. So get that out of your mind in case you had any idea of stopping and telling anyone about this. We know exactly how long it should take you to get where you're going, so no tricks, please. Now. Where are you?'

'I'm . . . I don't know.'

'All right, keep that phone in your hand. You are not to hang up until this trip is over. Keep it in your hand, and as you pass the next cross street, tell me where you are.'

'All right.'

'What is it?' Carella whispered. He was kneeling close to the back of his seat, his mouth alongside King's ear. King shook his head and pointed to the telephone.

'You think he'll hear us?' Carella whispered.

King nodded.

'I'm coming up front. I'll talk to him from now on. The reception on these damn things isn't hi-fi, that's for sure. We'll have to hope he doesn't recognize the change of voice. What does he want?'

'Cross street,' King whispered as Carella climbed over the seat and took the phone from King's hand. He looked through the windshield and then brought the receiver to his mouth.

'I'm approaching North Thirty-ninth and Culver,' he said into the phone.

Apparently, Eddie did not detect the difference in the voices. His own voice level and calm, he said, '*Turn left on North Fortieth. Continue in a southerly direction until you reach Grover Avenue, then turn left again. Go uptown until Forty-eighth, where you will see a crosstown entrance into the park. Take that entrance and continue driving. When you reach Hall Avenue, let me know. Have you got that?*'

'Left on North Fortieth,' Carella repeated. 'South until Grover, then left again. Uptown to Forty-eighth, and then into the park. Right.'

He covered the mouthpiece with his hand. 'Have you got that, King?'

'Yes,' King said.

'He's giving it to us piecemeal so we can't alert the nearest traffic cop as to just where we're heading. These are shrewd bastards, Mr King.' Carella's brow furrowed. 'I wish I knew how to stop them. I just wish I knew.'

Sitting in the parked car, Sy Barnard smoked his tenth cigarette in the past half hour. Anxiously, he looked at his watch. Then he glanced again at the road. The car was parked in the woods, completely shielded from the road by an old electric-company repair shack. The screening, in all truth, was unnecessary. Only one car had driven by in the past half hour, and on the day he and Eddie had chosen the site they had clocked only three cars in two and a half hours. The chances of being spotted by a curious motorist were negligible, almost nonexistent. Nor was there much possibility of a police car cruising by. Studying the list of road blocks, Sy knew that the nearest police barricade was at a big intersection some fifteen miles to the west. He had easily avoided it in getting here, and he knew he could easily go around it when driving back to the farmhouse.

Even if King refused to obey orders, even if, for example, a squad car were following the black Cadillac at this moment, the plan was still foolproof. And the part of it that made it so beautiful was the fact that no one but King knew where he was going, and even he was getting it in small bits and pieces so that he couldn't possibly give any meaningful information to a third party. The electric-company shack was just around a curve in the road. If a police car were following King, it would have to maintain a respectable distance or risk being detected. Detection would endanger the boy, and so Sy knew that any following police would stay pretty far behind the lead car. Communicating with King via the telephone, Eddie would know when King was about five miles away from the site. He would tell him to pull over to the side of the road and lower his right-hand window. Then he would tell King to begin driving again. At a point a half mile from the shack, Eddie would tell King that he was approaching a curve in the road. As soon as he rounded that bend, he wanted King to slow down, pull over, stop, and drop the carton of money out of the window and into the bushes on the right-hand side of the road. He was to drive away from the spot as quickly as possible then, following the instructions that came to him over the telephone.

And therein lay the beauty of the plan. A following squad car would be nowhere in sight when the drop was made. By the time they approached the electric-company shack, King would have driven off. They would continue to follow, not having witnessed the drop, not even knowing it had taken place. Eddie would continue talking to King. He would lead him out to the very tip of Sands Spit, turn him around at the end of the peninsula, and then lead him back to the city via another route. The following police car, if there was one, would continue tailing the lead car. Eddie would continue talking to King until Sy had picked up the money and driven back to the farmhouse. The moment Sy stepped through the door, Eddie would stop transmitting. King – and the police, if there were any – would then be on their own. They would be free to drive wherever the hell they wanted to. They could even drive back to the electric-company shack if they so chose; Sy would have left there long ago.

The plan, then, was beautiful.

And yet he was nervous.

He could not quell the persistent feeling that something would go wrong.

And yet he couldn't figure what.

He was not, you see, a Bible-reading man.

He did not know that the meek shall inherit the earth.

Studying the street map, Eddie Folsom said, 'All right, you're now approaching the Black Rock Span. There's a toll booth there, and the toll is a quarter, Mr King, twenty-five cents. Get the change out of your pocket now, and have it ready. Don't hand the attendant a hundred-dollar bill or anything like that to attract attention. And don't say anything to him. It won't do you any good at all to have police following you. If there are any cops when it comes time to make the drop, we'll call the whole thing off and kill the boy. Do you hear me, Mr King?'

'*Yes, I hear you*,' Carella answered.

'Good,' Eddie said. 'Go through the toll booth and onto the bridge. Let me know as you're driving off the bridge, and I'll tell you what to do next. It won't help to say anything to the cop collecting the toll because you still don't know where you're going. Any tricks, and we kill the boy.'

Listening to her husband, Kathy winced at the words.

Kill the boy.

Kill the boy.

My husband, she thought.

My fault.

In the automobile, Steve Carella reached into his back pocket and took out his wallet. He hastily opened it to where his shield was pinned to the leather. He unpinned the shield, took out his notebook rapidly scribbled:

Call police headquarters. Tell them King contacted by radio transmission to car telephone. Try to get a fix. Hurry!
Detective Steve Carella

He pinned his shield to the note, took a quarter from his pocket, and motioned King to pull over to the booth accepting quarters from the window opposite the driver's seat.

'*You at the booth yet, King?*' Eddie asked.

'Just approaching it.' Carella said.

'Have you got the change?'

'Yes, I've got a quarter.'

'*Good. No funny stuff.*'

The car slowed and pulled up alongside the toll booth. Carella handed the uniformed cop on duty a quarter, the note and his police shield. He nodded tersely at the cop as King pulled away and joined the steady stream of traffic moving across the bridge.

'You're coming off the bridge now, is that right?' Eddie asked.

'*That's right*,' Carella answered.

'Okay, bear to your left. I don't want you going out to Calm's Point. There's a big sign reading Mid-Sands Highway. That's the road I want you to take.'

Standing behind her husband, Kathy began to piece together a clear picture of what the markings on the street maps meant. The spot outlined with the red circle was obviously the Douglas King house, and the route marked in red was the route over which Eddie was leading him. The place marked 'Farm' was, of course, the farmhouse, situated on Fairlane Road, about a half a mile from Stanberry Road. And the spot marked with the blue star . . . ?

'Keep driving until you reach Exit Seventeen,' Eddie said. 'Have you got that, King?'

'*I've got it*,' Carella said.

The blue star confused Kathy because the red line went directly past it and then continued on out to the end of the peninsula, where it once again turned and headed back for the city. If the drop . . .

But of course.

The blue star indicated Sy's hiding place. They would ask King to drop the money and then keep him driving, simply to get him away from the spot or to confuse any followers. Of course. Sy Barnard, then, was lying in wait at . . .

She studied the map more closely.

. . . Tantamount Road, just around the curve in Route 127.

'Eddie,' she said.

'Not now, for God's sake!' he yelled, one hand cupped over the microphone.

'Eddie, let's get out of this. Please. Please.'

'No!' he said. 'Where are you now, King?' he asked into the microphone.

'Approaching Exit Fifteen,' Carella answered.

'*Let me know when you pass Sixteen*,' Eddie said.

'All right,' Carella covered the mouthpiece of the telephone.

'Where do you suppose he's leading us?' King asked.

'I don't know. Somewhere out on the peninsula.' He shook his head. 'If we knew that, Mr King . . .'

Sy Barnard looked at his watch again.

It shouldn't be long now. Come on, Eddie, he thought. Hurry them up. Get them over here with the gold. Let them make the drop, and let me pick it up, and let me get back to that farmhouse safely.

Come on. Please. Hurry up.

Sy didn't realize it, but he was praying.

'What do you make of this, Harry?' the uniformed cop asked.

The cop in the adjoining toll booth handed a motorist his change and said, 'What?'

'Lower that radio a minute, will you?'

'Sure.' He turned down the volume. 'What is it?'

'Guy just handed me this. What do you make of it?'

Harry studied the shield and the note. 'What do I make of it? You damn fool, this guy's a bull! Get on the phone right away!'

'How do you know he's legit?'

'Mister, you can't buy shields like that in the five and ten!'

'Headquarters, Detective Snyder.'

'Listen, this is Patrolman Umberson, shield number 63457, I'm in a toll booth on the Black Rock Span.'

'Yeah, what is it, Umberson?'

'A black Caddy just went through the toll stop. Guy handed me a badge and a note asking me to call Headquarters.'

'What kind of a badge?'

'Detective.'

'What's the number on it?'

'Just a second.' There was a pause on the line. 'Number 8712,' Umberson said.

'So what about it?'

'The note said to tell Headquarters that King was contacted by radio transmission to the car telephone. It said to try to get a fix. Does that make any sense to you?'

'King contacted by . . .' Detective Snyder shrugged. 'I just came on duty,' he said, 'It don't mean nothing to me. I'll check on that badge number, see if it's legitimate tin. What was the guy's name again?'

'King.'

'King, huh? Like the guy in that kidnapping over in

Smoke—' Snyder started and then suddenly said, 'Oh, my God!'

'Call it off, Eddie,' Kathy said. 'End it. We'll take the boy and—'

'I'm not calling anything off!' Eddie snapped. 'I have to do this, Kathy! I have to!'

'Please. If you love me, I'm asking you to . . .'

'*All right, we just passed Exit Seventeen*,' Carella said.

'Fine. Turn off at Seventeen and drive four blocks north. Then double back until you hit the parkway entrance below this one. You'll be heading in the opposite direction,' Eddie said. 'Drive down one exit to Exit Fifteen. Let me know when you—'

'The boy is in a farmhouse on Fairlane Road, a half mile from Stanberry!' Kathy suddenly shouted into the open microphone.

'What the hell—' Eddie started, and he turned to face her, but he was too late, the lid had blown, the words were spouting from her mouth.

'Sy Barnard is waiting in a car . . .'

'Kathy, stop it, are you crazy?'

'. . . on Tantamount Road, around the curve in 127.'

'Did you hear that?' Carella shouted.

'I heard it,' King said.

Carella slammed the receiver down onto the hook. 'Head for Tantamount Road, Route 127,' he said to King. 'Straight ahead, turn off at Exit Twenty-two. Step on it. Never mind the speed limit.' He lifted the receiver from the hook again and waited for the operator.

'Your call, please?'

'This is a police officer,' Carella said. 'Get me Headquarters immediately.'

'Yes, sir!' the operator said.

Sy Barnard was sitting in the automobile smoking his fifteenth cigarette when the black Cadillac rounded the bend in the road.

This is it, he thought. *This is it*.

The car slowed to a stop. The window on the right-hand side of the car was open. Sy watched, expecting to see a pair of hands appear at the window, expecting to see a carton of money drop into the bushes. Instead, the door opened and a man with a gun in his hand leaped out.

What the . . . ? Sy thought, and then he cursed Eddie for not having warned him somehow, and then stopped cursing because he realized it had been impossible to warn him, and then wondered what had gone wrong, and then turned the ignition key and started the car, and then ducked because that son of a bitch with the gun had opened fire. He drove straight for the man with the gun. The man kept firing. Two bullets shattered the windshield, but Sy drove past, seeing another man jump out of the Cadillac. The car had no sooner hit the macadam highway than Sy heard a fusillade of shots and felt the car give a sudden lurch, and knew at once that a tyre had been hit. The back window shattered and Sy figured he'd be better off on foot from here on in. He drove the limping car for another few yards, hopped out before it had stopped rolling, and began running into the woods.

The guy with the gun was reloading.

The other guy, a tall man with greying temples, began running after Sy.

Sy instantly drew his own pistol, turned, and fired twice, missing.

He thrashed into the woods.

'Give it up!' the man behind him yelled. 'We know where your partner is!'

'Go to hell!' Sy shouted, and he turned and fired again but the big man behind him did not slow his pace. He stamped into the woods after Sy and again Sy fired, and again, and suddenly the gun was empty. He threw away the useless pistol. He reached into his pocket, and the switch knife flashed into view, and suddenly the big man came around an outcropping of rocks, and Sy said softly, 'Hold it!'

'Hold crap!' Douglas King said, and he lunged.

The knife ripped upward, cutting a swath across King's overcoat. Again it slashed, digging deeper this time, tearing into King's jacket and running a thin line of blood across his flesh. King's hands tightened on Sy's throat.

'You son of a bitch! You lousy son of a bitch!' King muttered, his hands tightening, tightening, as he backed Sy against a tree. The knife flashed erratically now, searching for flesh. King's grip on Sy's throat would not loosen. A powerful man with hands that once had cut leather, he battered Sy's head against the tree, never relaxing his grip, silently, coldly, viciously pounding the other man until the knife dropped quietly from his lax fingers.

Exhausted, dizzy from the pounding, Sy Barnard only mumbled, 'Give . . . give me a break, will you?'

Douglas King didn't know the *Dragnet* answer. He held Sy until Carella came up with the handcuffs.

And that was that.

The patrolmen who responded to the call from Headquarters drove into the front yard of the farm and stopped the squad car. They drew their revolvers and took up positions flanking the door, listening. The house was silent. One patrolman cautiously tried the knob, and the door eased open.

An eight-year-old boy was sitting in the centre of an open sofa bed, a blanket draped over his shoulders.

'Jeff?' the patrolman asked.

'Yes.'

'You okay?'

'Yes.'

The patrolman studied the room. 'Anybody here with you?'

'No.'

'Where'd they go?' the second patrolman asked.

Jeff Reynolds hesitated a long time before answering. Then he said, 'Where'd *who* go?'

'The people who were holding you here,' the patrolman said.

'No people were holding me here,' Jeff answered.

'Huh?' the first patrolman said. He studied his black note pad. 'Look,' he said patiently, as if he were talking to a confused adult rather than a child, 'a detective named Carella called Headquarters from a car telephone. He said you were being held in a farmhouse on Fairlane, half a mile from Stanberry. Okay, so here you are. He also said a dame named Kathy had shouted the dope over a radio microphone, and that there was a guy with her. Now where are they, son? Where'd they go?'

'I don't know who you're talking about,' Jeff said. 'I've been all alone here ever since Sy left.'

The two patrolmen stared at each other.

'He must be in shock,' one of them said.

Jeff stuck to his story.

And, if life must have its little surprises, Sy Barnard corroborated the child's fable. He did not know whom the police were talking about, he said. He knew of no one named Kathy. He had engineered and executed the job singlehanded.

'You're lying and we know you're lying,' Lieutenant Byrnes said. 'Somebody had to be there to operate that transmitter.'

'Maybe it was a Martian,' Sy said.

'What the hell do you hope to gain by lying?' Carella asked. 'Who are you protecting? Don't you know the woman was the one who gave you away?'

'What woman?' Sy said.

'A woman named Kathy. The man yelled her name the minute she blew her stack.'

'I don't know any dame named Kathy,' Sy said.

'What's this, some code of yours? The law of the pack? No squealers allowed? *She told us exactly where we would find you. Barnard!*'

'I don't know who coulda told you, because I was in this alone,' Sy insisted.

'We'll get them, Barnard. With or without your help.'

'Will you?' Sy asked. 'I don't know how you're gonna get somebody that doesn't exist.'

'One thing makes me want to puke,' Parker said, 'is thieves who got honour.'

'So puke,' Sy said, and Parker hit him suddenly and viciously.

'What's the broad's last name?' Parker asked.

'I don't know who you mean!'

Parker hit him again.

'Kathy, Kathy,' Parker said. 'Kathy what?'

'I don't know who you mean,' Sy said.

'What are you selling us?' Parker said. 'You know damn well who . . .'

'I ain't selling you nothing,' Sy said.

Parker drew back his fist.

'Put away your hands, Andy,' Carella said.

I'd like to . . .'

'Put them away.' Carella turned to Sy. 'You're not doing yourself any good, Barnard, and you're not helping your pals, either. We'll get them. You're not giving them anything but time.'

'Maybe time is all they need,' Sy said, and there was a sudden sadness in his voice. 'Maybe a little time is all anybody ever needs.'

'Lock him up,' Byrnes said.

14.

IN THE SQUADROOM of the 87th Precinct, Detective Steve Carella typed up his final report on the Jeffry Reynolds kidnapping. It was a bitter-cold day at the end of November, and the steam rising from the cup of coffee on his desk gave a feeling of coziness to the otherwise drab squadroom. The feeble November sunshine sifted through the meshed grille-work covering the long windows, patched the floor in pale gold. Carella ripped the three copies of the report from the machine, separated them from the carbon copies, turned to Meyer Meyer and said, 'Finis.'

'End of story,' Meyer Meyer said. 'Steve Carella, star reporter for the *Isola Rag*, writes thirty to another dazzling assignment. Justice once more triumphs. Sy Barnard rots in jail. The police are jubilant. Another threat to the safety of John Q. Public is eliminated. Steve Carella, star reporter, lights a cigarette and meditates on crime and punishment, justice and the power of the press. Hooray for Carella, the crowd shouts. Long live Carella, the crowd roars. Carella for Presi—'

'Up yours,' Carella said.

'But what of those behind the scenes?' Meyer asked grandiosely. 'What of the mysterious woman known only as Kathy? What of the man who shouted her name into the transmitter microphone in that lonely deserted farmhouse? Where are they now? You might well ask,' Meyer said, 'because even the intrepid star reporter doesn't know.'

'Out of the country is my guess,' Carella said. 'I wish them luck.'

'What the hell for? Kidnappers?'

'Kids are like puppies,' Carella said. 'If Jeff Reynolds refused to bite somebody's hand, that hand must have been kind to him. That's the way I figure it. Who the hell knows what was behind all this, Meyer? Barnard isn't telling, and he never will. He'd rather get the chair than the mark of a squealer. His silence makes him a big man at Castleview Prison, the hoodlum the cops couldn't break. Okay, give the louse his day of glory. Maybe everybody's entitled to his day of glory.' Carella paused. 'Kathy. That's a nice name.'

'Sure. She must be a nice girl, too,' Meyer said. 'She only took part in a kidnapping.'

'We don't know the facts,' Carella said. 'Maybe she deserved what Jeff Reynolds gave her. Who knows?'

'Steve Carella's flintlike eyes softened,' Meyer said, 'for beneath the crusty exterior of this star reporter's breast there beat the heart of an old washerwoman,' Meyer sighed. 'Who do we whitewash next? Douglas King?'

'He got his lumps,' Carella said.

'He brought them on himself. You know what the bastard was most pleased about after all this was over? The fact that his damn stock deal went through and that he's going to be president of his lousy shoe company. Now how about that, Steve? Just how about that?'

'Some guys always pick up all the marbles,' Carella

said. 'His wife went back to him, you know that, don't you?'

'Sure. Why do the louses of the world always get the rewards?'

'While the good die young,' Carella finished for him.

'I ain't dead yet,' Meyer said.

'Neither is King. Maybe nobody got ransomed in this damn case, or maybe *everybody* did.'

'How's that again?' Meyer asked.

'Give the man time. He didn't have to stick his neck out against that switchblade.'

'Just because a guy has the guts to face a knife,' Meyer said, 'it doesn't necessarily mean he has the guts to face himself.'

'Pearls, pearls,' Carella said. 'Give him time. He figures he can't change. I figure he *has* to change, or he's dead. Why do you think his wife went back to him? Because he helps old ladies across the street?'

'Because she's got an investment in the louse, that's why,' Meyer said.

'Sure. But not in Granger Shoe, though. Her investment is in Douglas King. And she struck me as the kind of woman who knows when to sell a stock that's falling.'

'Careful or we'll switch you to the financial pages,' Meyer said.

'Whoo!' Andy Parker said from the gate in the slatted rail divider, slapping his arms at his sides, stamping into the room. 'If it gets much colder out there, I'm leaving for the South Pole.'

'What's the street like?'

'Cold.'

'I mean . . .'

'Who knows? You think I look for crime on days like this? I look for warm candy stores, that's what I look for.'

'Everybody changes, huh?' Meyer said. 'The day Andy Parker changes is the day I become a street cleaner.'

'You're a street cleaner already,' Parker said. 'Where'd you get that coffee, Stevie?'

'From Miscolo.'

'Hey, Miscolo!' Parker bellowed. 'Bring in the joe!'

'He'll have to pay it one day,' Carella said thoughtfully.

'Huh? Who'll have to pay what?' Parker asked.

'King,' Carella said. 'His *own* ransom.'

'I don't like riddles on cold days,' Parker said.

'Then why'd you become a cop?'

'My mother forced me.' He paused. 'Miscolo, where's the goddamn coffee?'

'Coming, coming,' Miscolo yelled back.

'I hate to file this,' Carella said, studying the report.

'Why?' Meyer asked.

'Maybe because I feel the case is still open. For a lot of people, Meyer, it's still open.'

Meyer grinned. 'You only *hope* it is,' he said, and the coffee came into the room, Miscolo staggering under the load of the cups and the huge pot, the aroma assailing the nostrils. The men poured and drank and told their dirty jokes.

Outside the squadroom, the city crouched.